URBAN WITCH

EVE LANGLAIS

Urban Witch © 2021/2022, Eve Langlais

Cover Art by DanielleFine.com © 2021

Produced in Canada

Published by Eve Langlais ~ www.EveLanglais.com

E ISBN: 978 177384 2585

Print ISBN: 9781 177 384 2592

ALL RIGHTS RESERVED

This story is a work of fiction and the characters, events and dialogue found within the story are of the author's imagination and are not to be construed as real. Any resemblance to actual events or persons, either living or deceased, is completely coincidental.

No part of this book may be reproduced or shared in any form or by any means, electronic or mechanical, including but not limited to digital copying, file sharing, audio recording, email and printing without permission in writing from the author.

1

I SUDDENLY BECAME A WITCH WHILE STILL attending college. It happened when I died from alcohol poisoning—only I didn't stay dead. The good doctors at St. Mary of Mercy revived my drunken ass.

It should be noted that I'd always assumed rumors of overdosing on booze were an urban legend. The daughter of an Irish father should never be taken down by too much whiskey.

Yet, it happened. The paramedics were called and retrieved my unconscious butt from a pool of my own vomit—comprised of pizza, Cheetos, and booze. A nurse later chastised me and claimed that I'd almost choked to death. Not likely given my strong gag reflex, which my ex-boyfriend could attest to. He was less than impressed when I spat his exuberance back at him. In my defense, I'd warned him. He'd thought it would be funny. It was. For *me* as I watched him screaming, the slimy jizz sliding down his cheek.

But back to that fatal college party. Despite being taken to the hospital, I'd slipped into an alcohol-induced coma, and my heart stopped.

Dead at twenty-two.

In the prime of my life, taken too soon, yet I didn't get a bright tunnel or stairs to Heaven—which I kind of appreciated, given my college ass wasn't into exercise. Forget meeting a being of light or standing before the pearly gates. Apparently, I didn't merit a proper welcoming committee.

In good—and surprising—news, I also didn't start burning in the flames of Hell or get dragged anywhere by demons. My grandmother would have been shocked. After all, she'd been saying that I had the devil inside me from a young age. She wasn't far from wrong. I had dated a guy for a while who'd called himself Diablo. Things didn't work out. See above where I spit on him.

Back to my death. I stood in a dark place, so dark I couldn't see my hand or even feel the ground underfoot. My voice echoed when I uttered a bold, "Yo!"

I didn't receive a reply, but I did get the sense that I wasn't alone. You know that feeling you get when you're in bed, thinking about that gap under it? Logically, you understand that it only has dust bunnies and socks, but at the same time, you just fucking know there's something under there waiting to grab your poor defenseless ankle. Or how about that scary anticipation you get when you open the closet door and expect something to jump out?

I got that same feeling as I stood in pure nothingness.

Someone watched me.

Judged me.

And I swear, they sighed.

What can I say? I was a disappointment to everyone, especially my mother, who always wanted a girly girl but got stuck with me instead. Rebellious, pierced, hair a different color every other month, not into dolls, makeup, or romantic comedies. Oh, and a slut who'd told my mom she could forget me ever having kids. I wasn't into the snotty noses, crying, and all that other crap people endured with their progeny.

If you thought I was a daddy's girl, though, think again. My dad was a factory worker, blue-collar all the way. A guy who loved football, beer, and fixing cars. Not that much fixing occurred as he and his buddies hung out in the garage, bottles or cans in hand, standing around the open hood of a mid-eighties Camaro. I didn't think they ever got grease on their hands. And fifteen years later, I knew for a fact the car wouldn't ever start. I'd sold some of the less obvious parts to fuel my addictions during high school—which, to everyone's surprise, I'd graduated. I was a fuckup, but not a dumb one. At least, most of the time.

The presence in my nothing place oozed an impatient feel. Also familiar.

I waved an invisible hand and muttered, "Yeah. Yeah. You're disappointed. Tell me something I don't know. Can we hurry this along? Judge me, and let's get this over with."

Would I go high or low? I'd not led an exemplary life, but at the same time, I hadn't killed anyone, either—that I knew of. However, as sins went, I was a firm proponent of the five-finger discount, mainly applied against greedy corporations that could afford it—my parents included.

For good deeds, while I didn't volunteer at soup kitchens or other shit, I did donate my hand-medowns to my local women's shelter. Who turned around and claimed my pants with artfully placed holes were worse than rags. Prudes.

The dark-place presence vibrated my very soul as if it tried to convey a message.

"You'll have to try talking because I have no idea what you're attempting to say." I mean, hello, I didn't speak omniscient being.

The humming intensified. Urgency. Danger. Faith.

In me.

I laughed. "Dude, you've got the wrong person." Unless... "Are you a demon?" Was something trying to possess me? I held out my invisible arms and said, "Take me, oh mighty dark creature, and let's wreak havoc on the world."

I was actually joking. Mostly. So imagine my surprise when something slammed into me. Not my body, but my soul. It burned through me, and I screamed. It didn't hurt, but it *did* violate every inch of my being.

By the time whatever-the-fuck-it-was withdrew, I'd lost my cockiness. Even sulked a bit as I said, "Well, that was fucking rude."

I could have sworn the presence oozed smugness.

"What did you do to me?"

The presence didn't provide an answer.

"Well, this has been fun, but I think I'm done. What's next? Heaven? Hell? Shall we do an eeny, meeny, miny, moe to choose a winner?"

Rather than reply, the darkness around me spun.

Here we go. Moment of truth. Where would I end up?

What I didn't expect was to be spat back out into the world. Apparently, not dead, after all.

I woke to bright lights over me. People yapping. Machines beeping, and some doctor compressing my chest.

A cute one. So was it any wonder I slurred, "Hey, good-looking?"

It would have probably been sexier without the barf.

2

My *Exorcist* moment was followed by gagging because bile was fucking gross. The nurse who remained behind was kind enough to give me a glass of water to wash out my mouth. As I swirled and spat in a basin they provided, I got an earful about my condition.

"...were in a coma, and your heart stopped. We were actually about to call time of death when you revived."

"Because Hell rejected me," I muttered, a little miffed because, when even the devil didn't want you, what the fuck? Should I sin more to attract his notice? Less and see if I could regain a way into Heaven?

"Given the length of time your heart stopped beating, you'll need to be checked for brain damage."

I blinked at her. "My brain is fine. Would you like me to recite the alphabet backwards?" A skill I'd learned as a great way to mess with cops who asked if I'd had too much to drink. Speaking of which... "I could use a drink." I rubbed at my face, wondering if my waterproof mascara had survived my less-than-stellar night. Barf, raccoon eyes, and who knew what else. I must be super pretty right about now.

The nurse handed me a cup of water.

I grimaced. "Got anything stronger?"

"You're kidding, right?" The nurse, name tag *Marge*, ogled me.

"My mouth tastes like something shit in it. Fucking right, I want something with flavor." I swung my legs over the edge of the bed, noticing we were in a curtained area of the emergency department.

The cute doctor I'd splattered had disappeared, probably to change. Now that I was conscious, the other nurses and staff had other people to deal with, leaving me with just Marge, who crossed her arms and said, "Get back in that bed."

"No thanks. I'd rather sleep in mine."

"You can't leave yet. We need to check you over."

"I am not staying. I feel fine." Still a bit drunk, actually. I'd have one hell of a hangover when it wore off.

"There's still paperwork to do before you can go anywhere."

And she meant it, too. When I tried to sneak out, Marge practically tackled me to shove a clipboard at my face. Some of the info they'd already filled out, having found my student identification in my pocket.

Between signing, I endured a lecture on the dangers of drinking too much, the doctor's fresh coat tempting me to be a bit of a bitch. If I wanted to be harangued about my lifestyle, I'd call my parents.

After the doc's unsuccessful attempt to get me to agree to sobriety, a counselor swung by to give me a pamphlet offering rehab. It went into the trash.

I didn't have a drinking problem. I had a dare issue. As in someone dared me to chug? I said yes. From now on, I'd only get wasted the proper way, by taking actual sips and not siphoning through a funnel.

Only once I'd given them some way to collect payment—thanks to dear old Dad and his insurance—did Marge finally let me walk out the emergency room doors.

Freedom! But no money for a cab. Meaning, I had to walk back to the dorm.

Clunk. Clunk. My combat boots had definitely gotten heavier. I swore those nurses put weights in them. My clothes at least didn't show most of my ordeal. An accomplished puker, I knew to spew away from myself.

My mouth remained sour, and my head throbbed as the booze wore off. The clearing of my head meant remembering I had a paper due in just over a day. Not that it mattered if I handed it in or not. I was failing. At life. College. And now, drinking.

Just wait until my parents got the bill for the ambulance ride in the mail. At least my dad's insurance from work would cover the incident, but it wouldn't save my ears from a proper blistering.

As I passed an alley, a strange sound caught my ears. I turned and blinked. Obviously, still more drunk than I thought because there was no way I saw a short dude with green skin climbing into the dumpster. Probably a rat.

More rats peered at me through sewer grates, freaking me out with their red eyes. I could admit it was my first time ever seeing them do that. Apparently, almost dying caused an acid-like effect. I was seeing things. So, like any smart girl who'd overindulged, once I reached my dorm, I threw myself onto my bed and passed out—the sleeping kind, not coma-dead.

When I finally returned to the land of the living, this time without being molested by an invisible presence, it was to find myself stinking of sour sweat and tangled in my sheets. Gross, even by my standards.

At least my roommate, who chose to sleep most nights with her boyfriend, wasn't there to roll her eyes. Forget all those cutesy movies everyone gobbled up about the mismatched roomies becoming best friends. Katia hated me, and I was just indifferent. I was sure Katia would have switched rooms if not for the fact that I scored the best dope, including the pills she liked to pop before tests.

College was a joke. The majority of us didn't learn shit. We just cheated and faked our way into getting passing grades. I was sure a few nerds actually understood the gobbledygook coming out of our professors' mouths, but for the most part, we were merely trying to pass to get that vaunted diploma so we could go on to shitty jobs not in our field to pay off a never-ending student loan for a degree that didn't do shit.

So why go to college?

They had the best parties.

Pouring myself out of bed—AKA falling on the floor because gravity hated me—meant seeing under my bed where a bottle of juice had rolled and, beside it, a little purple lizard with kaleidoscope eyes. Blinking didn't make it disappear; rather it flicked a tongue at me. Since purple lizards didn't exist, I ignored it and reached for the juice, which turned out to be apple. The lukewarm sweetness removed some of the pastiness from my mouth but did little else to help.

I groaned. I'd need more than piss-warm juice to fix this hangover. Pity I'd not found a bottle of hooch —hair of the dog and all that.

The imaginary lizard remained, staring at me from under the bed. I shoved to my knees and blinked at my clock. Nine a.m. Surely, I'd slept more than a few hours.

Locating my phone didn't help as it had died. Great. As I plugged it in, I brushed my teeth at the tiny sink in the room. Then, not in the mood to navigate the hall, I squatted over it and peed. *Classy, I know.* You should see my skill at peeing upright and not getting any on my feet.

My phone had enough charge to boot up, and I had a moment of disbelief as I realized I'd been asleep longer than expected. Three days to be exact.

Three, with no one even checking on me. I could have died. *Wait, I did*. And nobody cared. That, more than anything, caused me to have a bit of a meltdown.

Was I that unlikeable?

Thinking about how I had a habit of pushing people away? Yes, yes, I could be. But I could also be loving and kind. My best friend through school knew that, but after she'd gone off to a different college, we'd lost touch. She had a new circle of people she hung out with now, and I'd not really found anyone I clicked with. It seemed crazy that, on a campus of hundreds, I couldn't connect with anyone.

The whisper of someone sliding paper under the door drew my attention. I blew at a hank of greasy hair and squinted as if I could read the tiny type on the envelope. In the end, I crawled over and snared the missive, addressed to me, Faye Bronson, with the college logo stamped on the back.

I remained sitting on the floor while reading it.

Apparently, my latest stint at the hospital, combined with my grades and the fact that I'd told my history professor to suck my juicy clit when he gave me an *F* for my Satan paper—he'd asked us to write about a historical person who'd affected the world—were the final straws.

Expelled. Effective immediately.

Fuck. Fuck. Fuck. FUCK!

My parents would freak.

Whoosh.

The sheet of paper in my hand ignited. I dropped it to the floor and watched it burn.

Pretty. Even as I wasn't sure how it got set on fire. I blamed my hazy mind for not recalling lighting it.

I packed my stuff, which was a fancy way of saying I filled a large, black garbage bag with my dirty clothes and a few personal effects. I slung it over my shoulder and headed out the door.

Forget saying goodbye. Who would care? I certainly didn't. I hated this place.

Hated. It.

Fuck all the asshole professors and the stuck-up students. Double fuck to the perky ones. I hated perky girls. Always happy and smiling. Judging me because I dared to have my own style.

Fuck them all. As far as I was concerned, they could all burn in Hell.

As I walked away from my dorm, I heard a bell start clanging. I whirled around to see smoke billowing out of the building I'd recently called home.

I stood and watched as people ran screaming. When my wobbly legs tired, I sat on my bag of shit and watched as the windows blew out, and flames spilled through the openings. I lost interest once the firefighters arrived and put out the fire.

Spoilsports.

News reports claimed they never discovered the cause. But, in good news, no one blamed me.

3

I had little money in my pockets, and none left in my bank account. Given my level of thirst, I hit the closest convenience store, shoplifting a hard cider and paying for a pack of gum. A cheap price to pay to avoid an over-eager store clerk coming after me.

The gum went into a pocket as I concentrated on twisting off the cap of the alcoholic cider and taking a long sip.

It was when I went to swallow that shit went awry. The liquid spewed right back out of me.

A second gulp also hit the pavement. I frowned at the bottle, and my mouth puckered at the residual flavor in my mouth. It tasted like ass. I didn't want to discuss how I knew that.

Probably a bad batch. Rare, but it happened. I tossed the bottle and chewed a piece of gum, the mint chasing away the gross.

As it turned out, it wasn't just that bottle of cider that wouldn't stay down. The beer I stole also made a repeat appearance. The red wine. Even the prissy cooler. Every single thing with alcohol I tried to drink to numb my annoyance refused to stay down.

Annoying because it meant that I was sober and very much aware of the looks aimed in my direction as I wandered aimlessly.

The hospital must have done something to me. Given me some kind of pill or injection to make my body reject booze.

Don't be crazy. Logically, I knew if such a thing existed, we'd no longer have alcoholics in the world. Must be my body telling me it needed more time to recover. After all, I *did* technically die.

Digging into my pocket for the last of my gum, I found a piece of foil. I practically collapsed in relief as I found a nugget of hash.

Goodbye, sober world. Time to get high and make everything all better.

It was easy to bum a smoke, especially given I snatched it from a guy who'd just lit one and took a drag. When I offered it back—after wetting the filter with my spit—he grimaced and said to keep it.

A plastic bottle I'd scored from a garbage can provided the makeshift bong. Piece of hash on the end of the cigarette, tip in the hole I'd made in the bottle, and then sucking out the smoke.

The medicinal aspect filled my mouth and then my lungs. A second later, I was hacking and coughing like a virgin after her first cigarette.

Fuck me. That was embarrassing. I put another little piece of the brown resin on the tip of the cigarette, sucked in some more smoke. Coughed so hard that I threw up a little in my mouth.

My throat burned. My lungs ached. I stared mournfully at the dope that had failed me when I needed it most.

So unfair. I just wanted a little buzz to take off the edge.

Alas, it wasn't meant to be.

My inability to get high left me irritable, especially as the day waned, and I realized I had nowhere to go. I called a few acquaintances, looking for a place to crash. One after another, the people I'd scored dope for or partied with on numerous occasions had an excuse for why I couldn't sleep on their couch for the night.

Eventually, I ended up slumped against a wall, out of ideas. Tired. Cranky. In no mood for the purple lizard that appeared and stared at me, kaleidoscope eyes unblinking.

"I'm beginning to think someone laced my drinks the other night," I muttered. Acid? LSD? Something I'd never heard of that had me seeing things days later?

"Where do you think I should go?" I asked my lizard companion. Perhaps this product of my subconscious would have an idea.

It flicked its tongue.

"You're not much help," I muttered.

With no options left, I had to do the thing I dreaded most.

I had to go back home.

4

Not being a complete idiot, in spite of all the drugs, I didn't call my parents to warn them that I was coming. I just showed up on the doorstep—after a very unnerving hitchhiking trip across a few states. When Mom opened at my knock, I offered a sheepish, "Surprise!"

Her lips pinched. "Not really. We figured you would be coming here after what happened."

No hug. No checking if I was okay. It led to me being a little sour with my reply. "I'm fine, thanks for asking." Although that guy who offered me a ride at the truck stop? Not fine given his car smoked with shooting flames the last time I saw it. Good timing, considering he'd been trying to force himself on me just before it ignited. *"You owe me, slut."* The only thing I owed him was a big, "Fuck you, asshole."

"Fine? Is that what you call what you've been doing with your life?" My mother and I had a rocky relationship, never more apparent than now.

Exhausted, I really didn't want to deal with her. "Can we discuss this later? It was a shitty trip." I'd hitchhiked most of the way due to a lack of cash. It meant slapping a few wandering hands, and in the case of the name-calling fellow, spilled out of the car a minute before the flames shooting out from under the hood spread.

"A trip that came about because of your expulsion from college."

"You heard?"

Her lips flattened in disapproval.

"Did you also hear that I ended up in the hospital?"

"And whose fault is that?" She arched a brow in a way that made me feel ashamed.

"You know, you could show a little more compassion. I almost died."

"Because you were drunk. Again." The words emerged soft and not yelled. Still, a chill went through me. Mom was always the most dangerous when she got quiet.

To look at her, you'd think her a lovely suburban housewife. Her hair always in a perfect bob with blonde highlights. She went to the salon every eight weeks like clockwork. She wore slacks, blouses, cardigans. Her idea of *comfortable* clothes usually involved a matching tracksuit that never saw sweat. In direct contrast to my dad and me, she didn't drink at all—and she could be so judgmental about that.

"So what if I had a few too many?" I muttered. "Not a big deal."

"The doctor I spoke to said you were legally dead."

She knew and still no hug? It hurt, and I lashed out with my usual sarcasm. "I can see you're just heartbroken about it."

"What did you expect, Faye? You've always been difficult. Even more so once you hit your teenage years. Doing whatever you wanted. A complete disregard for consequences. No regard for those you hurt."

"Excuse me for not being some perfect little doll you could dress up and show off to your friends," I snapped right back.

"I didn't expect you to be a perfect daughter, but you could have at least made an effort. Everything you do is about shocking people."

"You're the one who raised me."

"Don't you blame me for your recklessness."

No, I couldn't blame her because she'd spent my entire life trying to get me to conform and follow rules. I couldn't help rebelling against the institution, and it'd almost killed me.

"Well, I learned my lesson this time."

"I highly doubt that. And I'm tired of answering the phone and wondering what you've done to get in trouble. Arrested for breaking and entering? Shoplifting? In the hospital because you were drinking and did something dumb like jumping off a bridge?"

"I was fine afterwards." Only swallowed a little bit of the dirty river water.

Mom shook her head. "I can't do it anymore."

"What's that supposed to mean?" She was my mother. She had to forgive me.

"I'm done."

My stomach knotted. Mostly in shame because she was justified in her exasperation. I'd been a shit person. Especially to her. "I know I'm a major fuckup. I can't seem to make good choices."

"Enough with the excuses, Faye. It's time you faced real consequences for your actions."

"I almost died. I'd say I already did." A sour reminder for some sympathy that failed.

"Take responsibility for once in your life."

"I will. I promise. Turn over a new leaf and all that. Starting with finding a job."

"Sure, you will. Eventually. After much nagging by me. And then you'll find a reason to quit or be fired," my mother opined.

A rebuttal seemed appropriate; only once more, she was right. I never held on to any job for long. In my defense, all my managers were assholes. "I'll find something I like this time. You'll see."

"I won't hold my breath." The dry lack of faith hurt, but it was my fault she had no reason to believe me.

"I'll show you. First thing in the morning, I'll be pounding the pavement and applying."

"Good luck." Spoken as she started to close the door.

Hold on a second. What was happening here? "Um, Mom, I need a place to stay."

"Not here, Faye. We're done supporting you. It's time you grew up and took care of yourself."

The very idea had me in a panic. "I made a mistake."

"A series of them. Over and over, Faye."

Once more, I threw the pity card. "I almost died."

"Because you're out of control. I can't do it anymore." The façade finally cracked, the last words spoken on a tremble as if my mom choked back tears.

It hit me then that she did this because she cared. Because she couldn't stand to watch me destroying myself.

The door shut, and I heard the lock engage, leaving me outside, smacked with the realization that I'd finally pushed my parents too far. I knew better than to try going around Mom's decree to my dad. He never went against my mother. He always took her side against me.

Which was unfair. Not my fault that I inherited his drinking gene. I didn't see Mom freaking on him because he liked to pound back a few.

Then again, he'd never ended up in the hospital or the back of a cop car.

I stared at the door of my childhood home, repainted a few times—usually because of me. I'd carved my initials in it at fourteen. At sixteen, someone had written a nasty word that made my mother blanch and had my father up sanding and painting all night. The word was meant for me, of course.

Currently, the door was blue, a deep color that matched the shutters. A cute little house in rural fucktown. Where I wasn't welcome, making me homeless.

Whatever. Wouldn't be the first time I'd spent a night on the streets. I'd gotten wasted a few times and woken up in alleys, once on a picnic table at the park with a fresh-faced family gaping at me.

What I didn't count on? It was one thing to be passed out while drunk and/or high. Quite another to do it sober. The rain started as I trudged, looking for...I didn't even know. Where could I go? Our small town didn't have a shelter like the big city, but we *did* have a bridge.

Could I be more cliché? At the same time, a bridge meant protection from the rain. What I didn't expect but should have, was the fact that I might not be the only person who'd think of it.

A homeless throng already hung out, five men and one woman. Given the only female hissed in my direction, I swung a wide berth to the opposite side, heading for the barrel exuding heat from the fire someone had set in it.

A man with leathery skin, the kind formed over decades of being outside and smoking cigarettes, stepped in front of me. "Whatcha want?"

"To get warm."

"Cost you a quarter."

I thought about arguing against his shakedown and yet, at the same time, admired his capitalism.

I dug into my pocket for a coin. He eyed it and then me before cackling, showing off the gaps where he'd lost teeth to rot.

"Not that kind of quarter, girlie."

"If I had drugs, do you think I'd be here?" I'd have sold some to rent a room or smoked it to forget that I wasn't sleeping under a roof.

"You can't stay if you don't pay," the homeless dude sang.

"Says who? You?" I might be able to take him. I definitely outweighed his scrawny ass, but he had crazy on his side and possibly a few friends.

"The trollman is coming. You'd better pay your dues or else," he cackled.

"Who is the trollman?"

"The one who decides who gets to live under his bridge."

I snickered. "Someone's read *Billy Goats Gruff*."

"Mock while you can. He's coming, and those who haven't paid don't stay."

"Who made him boss?"

"It's his bridge."

Translation: This trollman had scared folks into thinking they needed permission. Made me kind of curious to meet him. Although, with a name like *troll*, I didn't expect to be wowed.

"How about I deal with this trollman when he comes, and you mind your business where I'm concerned?" I knew better than to be cowed by his demands. Act weak and get treated like a victim.

For a moment, the gap-toothed fellow held himself stiffly as if he debated pushing the issue. Then he grinned. "Suit yourself."

He turned away from me, and I tucked myself against the stone of the bridge footing, sitting on my bag because losing my grip on it, even for a second, might see it stolen.

Hunger hadn't hit me yet, and if it did, I still had a crushed bag of Doritos in there somewhere and a half bottle of water. I really wanted a drink. Maybe one of the kind folks not currently trying to shake me down would spare me a swig if I asked nicely. But I drew the line at hand jobs for a chug. Especially since I wasn't yet sure I'd be able to keep any booze down.

The ground under my butt trembled. Stopped. Shivered again. Stopped. I glanced around, but no one else reacted to it, making it normal. Or did I hallucinate still?

Over the three days of travel it'd taken to get home, I'd had episodes. For example, during the short-lived bus ride I'd bought a ticket for, I could have sworn I saw a gremlin crawling under the rig as I sat in the back waiting to leave. Within fifty miles, we were on the side of the road, waiting for a replacement bus.

Then there was the weirdness I'd encountered in the public bathroom I'd picked to sleep in for a night. I'd changed stalls because the one I'd chosen glowed around the seat as if it were possessed or some kind of portal.

Then there was my lizard friend, who kept reappearing. I'd named it Polkie, mostly because it seemed to always show itself just when I was ready to give up. Seeing it tended to nudge me into action. Maybe he was like my guardian gecko. If so, where the fuck was he?

Polkie remained hidden as the ground shook, as if something approached with thundering, ponderous steps. I expected a giant, maybe even some robot or a monster. Into the firelight, which barely dispelled the darkness, a person appeared, short—way shorter than me—dressed in Elvis finery from the sequined pants to the oversized sunglasses and sideburns.

Given how those under the bridge practically bowed as he passed, I assumed this had to be the trollman. Not very impressive if you asked me, an opinion revised as he stood in front of me and breathed. I practically died at the stench.

"Who is this under my bridge?" His voice had a lower timbre than expected.

"Just your run-of-the-mill college dropout," I quipped.

His nostrils flared as he sniffed. "What's this I smell?" he asked, leaning close, his breath a spew of noxious fumes.

My eyes watered. "Dude, a toothbrush. Learn to use one."

"Insults raise the price." He held out his hand.

"About that. I have nothing of value, obviously, or I wouldn't be here." I remained seated, making me almost at eye-level with him.

"Pay." An imperious demand.

"Are you listening? I have nothing." Up close, his face proved lumpy, his eyes not equidistant, his nose broad and hooked.

He flexed his hand, grimy with dirt, in direct contrast to his clean suit. As I stared, I could have sworn his fingers went from stubby sausages to massive green appendages tipped in claws.

A blink, and it was back to being a demanding hand.

I dropped the original quarter I'd dug free onto his palm. The short man closed his fist around it.

"Not enough."

"How much is it to stay, then? And what amenities are you offering? I don't suppose you offer a continental breakfast?"

"You mock me," he huffed, and I almost gagged at the stench.

"Wow, you must be a hit with the ladies."

"No pay. No stay," he announced.

"I paid. Now go away." I shooed him with a wave of my hand.

"Oooh." I swear all the homeless hummed in unison.

The trollman's face rippled. "You are not welcome, witch."

"Name-calling now? How mature. This bridge is public property. You don't own it."

"It's mine," he growled.

I stood and towered over him. "I don't really care. I'm staying."

"No, you're not."

"And how're you going to make me leave?"

Apparently, by dragging me out. His hand wrapped around me, the stubby fingers appearing to only half grab me. And yet, my flesh thought a massive hand gripped. A strong one that pulled me along without choice.

5

I protested. "Hey, let go."

Trollman didn't listen and handled me in a way that made no sense. Because he shouldn't have had the size or strength to drag me out from under the bridge, thrusting me into the downpour.

Immediately, I got soaked head to toe and shivered from the cold. Maybe I should have been a little nicer.

"Can't we talk about this?" As I stared at him, he suddenly went from a short Elvis to a hulking monster with tusks that grunted, "No."

I blinked, and he remained a giant-sized troll, who turned around and stomped back under the bridge, each step causing a tremble.

Given I appeared to be in the midst of some

psychedelic episode, it might be best to do it away from people. Nothing worse than passing out and waking up with your clothing scattered and wondering what'd happened.

With quick steps, I moved from the bridge into the main part of town—if you could be so grand about a dozen interconnected streets. I wandered until I found an alley with a dry strip along one wall. I huddled there and slept.

I proceeded to have the strangest dream. I didn't sail to China, but in my dream, I did want to get my laundry clean. As the song *Break My Stride* played in my head, I suddenly found myself in front of a dry cleaner, the window for the business promising same-day service for a premium. As if I'd ever pay extra. Being a cheap-ass student, I didn't ever use dry cleaners. I crammed the biggest load I could into the industrial coin machines on campus and stole other students' soap. The time I couldn't get a hold of any, I'd tried using the hand soap found in public washrooms, but the suds it created caused a problem with management.

I stared at the store, strangely compelled to go inside. Why? I had no reason. Yet my hand gripped the handle and tugged at the door, swinging it open and setting off a tiny bell.

Inside, a mature woman—forties, maybe a touch older, with dark hair pinned atop her head—perched on a stool behind the counter. She peered at me through glasses perched on the tip of her nose.

"Well, you're certainly not what I expected," she declared with a slight accent.

An odd thing to say. But then again, this was a dream. Shit didn't have to make sense.

"I don't know why I came in. I don't have anything for you to clean."

"Are you sure about that?" Disdain was clear as she eyed me, and not just my attire. She appeared disapproving of my entire look.

If I could handle my father's scowl and my whole extended family's disparaging remarks, then who cared about a stranger?

"You like?" I did a twirl to show off my favorite metal band T-shirt and worn jeans with the back pocket partially ripped off. My pink hair whirled with me.

By the time I faced the woman again, she had pursed lips. "How old are you?"

"You first."

"Old enough to know you are not what this city needs."

"Wow, that's pretty judgy, given we barely just met."

"I've seen enough. I prayed for help, not a mouthy child."

I snorted. "Wow, your god must hate you." I didn't mention that Satan himself didn't want anything to do with *me*. I'd died and been rejected. That still stung. But not as much as my mother finally turning her back on me.

"Do you ever think before you speak, child?"

"Hardly a kid, as I can legally drink."

"Too much, apparently." Again, I had to endure the whole disapproving bit. Even in my dreams, I couldn't escape it.

I stuck out my tongue. Also pierced. Like my nose. Ears. Navel. I'd almost had my clit done, but I was a horny girl who masturbated regularly and, given I was advised that it took a bit to heal, decided against it—for now. My nipples, though? Hell, yeah, they had hoops.

As if the old lady had read my mind, she tsked. "Something obviously went wrong with my spell," she mused aloud.

"That fake virgin's blood will get you every time," I mocked.

"Definitely awry," she muttered.

Which stung. Even in my dreams, I couldn't get any respect.

"Why exactly are you praying for help?" I asked.

"None of your business."

"You're the one who mentioned it."

"Would it matter if I told you? Would you even care if I said the fate of many depends on you? You're selfish, hardly the type to volunteer."

"Guess you got me pegged, lady." I was offended, even as what she surmised was true. I *didn't* work for free. I preferred dealing in cash so Uncle Sam didn't steal a cut.

"Begone. You waste my time."

And with that, she blew me out of her store. Like, literally. She opened her mouth wide and huffed, hard enough that I slammed into the door and onto the street before shooting straight up.

Oh, shit! I was flying.

I was—

6

My dream flight ended in a painful face-plant onto the pavement, which would have been bad enough, but there also happened to be some old gum there. At least, I hoped it was gum. I scrubbed my nose clean of it as I sat and blinked. No freaky lady and no dry-cleaning store.

Talk about some vivid dreaming. Even rarer, I actually remembered it.

I stood, and my stomach immediately grumbled. It needed food. Problem being, I still had no cash, and no options.

I debated going home and trying again. Maybe my mom had spent the night letting her guilt over her treatment of me mount. Her anger might have died off, and perhaps she'd relent and at least let me stay a few days until I got on my feet.

If I'd had something to dull my anxiety, I would have gone back. Drugs and booze had a way of taking my self-respect. But I remained stone-cold sober. Had been since my stint in the hospital.

Not for lack of trying. And the fact that I couldn't, more than anything, scared the shit out of me. What'd happened to me? Yes, I'd died, but something *else* occurred, and it had changed me in ways I'd yet to truly understand.

For one, my mind kept playing tricks on me. A week since my death, and I continued to see the impossible—monsters and strange lights. Let's not forget my purple companion, Polkie.

Of more concern, fires kept popping up in my vicinity. It reminded me of that old Stephen King story, the one they made into a movie. Was it me starting fires with the power of my mind or just a coincidence? A part of me wasn't sure I wanted to know.

Standing in the gross alley, I stretched, and joints popped. I could have used a shower and a change of clothes, yet that remained out of reach. I couldn't go home, nor could I stay here. How to leave, though? I had no money, no car, and my grumbling belly reminded me that it had been a while since we'd eaten. I needed to do something about that.

The grocery store provided the opportunity. I five-fingered an apple and some pepperoni sticks. I also bumped into a woman. Her wallet, lying out in the open atop her purse while shopping, was easy to slide into my pocket. A twinge of remorse hit when a kid yelled "Mom!" as I walked away.

Dammit. I pulled only a twenty from the wallet before dropping it in an aisle to be easily found later. It was enough for a bus ticket into the city—chosen because Polkie flicked his tongue at the destination.

Why not follow the advice of my imaginary pet? At least he had a plan.

Arriving at the city's main bus terminal, I decided not to stay long. Not once I saw the pair of roaming security guards sporting lizard heads—great big grey-green ones, not cute and purple. The lizard people with their thick tails appeared invisible to everyone but me. They were also quite populous.

Everywhere I went, giant reptiles walked on two legs, many in uniform, others as civilians mixing among the normal folk. The city appeared infested, or so my beleaguered mind convinced me. It made it hard to know where to stare when I had to finally speak with one. I expected them to lisp or maybe catch a fly with that forked tongue. Instead, the lizard person handed me my change and a burger.

I couldn't stay here. I moved onto another city after doing a stint on the pole. *Don't judge.* Stripping was the quickest way to make cash, and it only involved taking off my clothes.

Again, totally different when sober. For my first set, I was a nervous wreck as I eyed the crowd, a few of them with lizard heads, which turned out to be less freaky than the guy with a single giant eye in his forehead.

The crowd leered at me. Made me feel dirty to the point where I scooped my money and practically ran. My gorge rose as I dressed, remembering the drunken times I'd willingly given lap dances for twenty dollars a pop and a grope for a few bucks more.

I wished I could claim I titillated men for a noble reason in the past. But alas, my only thought was to party and find ways to get fucked up.

It stunned me to realize that this was the longest I'd gone without a drink or a toke. I'd started at twelve and now closed in on twenty-three.

Eleven years of ruining my health. Of straining and finally severing all ties.

Being straight meant being able to actually

analyze the things I'd done and said—most of them bad. How had Hell rejected me when I died? I certainly didn't return as some kind of religious nut. Still didn't really believe in God, even as I thought the devil did exist. I had no urge to pray for forgiveness. How could I even start to ask, knowing the pain I'd caused?

A tiny violin played as I wallowed. I also frowned. Usually, the self-pity drove me to drink or dope. Since I remained unable to imbibe either, I had to live with my choices. And make better ones if I didn't want them to haunt me in the future.

The next city I traveled to—once more chosen by Polkie, who flicked his tongue at the name—proved to be the biggest so far. And while some of the folks didn't appear as they should, my hallucinating brain pegged the majority as human.

Out of cash, I began walking, not aimlessly given Polkie chose to scuttle ahead of me, his cute little tail wiggling behind him. My mouth watered as I passed the breakfast joints with their brewing coffee and fresh pastries. The bakery almost made me cry. Nothing like a fresh croissant to start the day.

While someone fixed their coffee at the cream and sugar counter, I snared their unattended paper bag. It contained a healthy muffin, which, while not my favorite, hit the spot. I ignored Polkie's disapproving stare.

Midmorning during my aimless trek—because Polkie didn't seem to have any rhyme or reason to his wandering—I noticed I was being followed. I'd been practically window licking a place with the most amazing display of cookies when I caught his reflection.

A tall dude, skinny, with spiked, bright red hair. He wore a plaid lumberjack coat and big boots. He turned his head and caught me looking. I could have sworn his eyes turned into two glowing coals as he bared teeth sharpened into points.

Freaky, and not someone I wanted to tangle with.

I ducked around the side of a building then fast-walked to the end of that block and turned again. I flattened myself against the wall around the corner and waited.

Sure enough, a few minutes later, a red-haired dude stuck his head around, looking. His eyes widened when he spotted me.

Too late to avoid my fist.

7

My fist smashed the red-haired stalker's kisser hard enough to snap his head back and break bone.

"Argh," he yelled, slapping a hand to his nose.

"Serves you right. Perv! Stay away, or I will really fuck you up," I warned. And I meant it. I wondered if my parents were surprised to discover that it was my drinking and not my propensity for violence that had gotten me expelled from college. After all, previous incidents had led to me moving to three different schools growing up. A short temper and hormones were a bad combination. It didn't help that my father taught me to spar. Add in a few dirty tricks to even the odds in my favor because I never got heavier than a hundred and thirty pounds even soaking wet, and...

The stalker reached for me. Men never did listen.

I knocked aside his hand, and my foot hit him in the crotch. He folded with a gasp.

It was my chance to move; however, I had an issue with his actions. I shook a finger in his face. "This is not the Dark Ages, asshole. You do not follow women and act creepy. I won't be a victim. You should be ashamed of yourself."

"Witch," he hissed.

"Of course, you'd resort to shit talk when you're called out for being a creep."

A low growl rumbled from him.

I shook my fist. "Want another?"

Rather than reply, he slunk away, moving in a disjointed fashion that somehow avoided notice by the people on the sidewalk. But they stared quite frankly at me and offered me a wide berth as if I were contagious.

People these days. They couldn't be counted on to do the right thing anymore. No one wanted to get involved—that included me.

Fired up, I hoisted my bag higher, the plastic

digging into my grip, and stomped. Head down and muttering, I gave people a reason not to come closer.

What am I going to do?

I couldn't wander forever. I needed to find food and some kind of room to stay in. I really should be looking for a job. But who would hire me, stinking of the streets? Where could I go? A city this size might have a homeless shelter. Not a great place for a woman, yet I had no other choices.

Polkie abruptly disappeared, and I paused, my garbage bag of stuff hitting the sidewalk, my shoulders drooping. If only my mom hadn't been such a bitch and tossed me out.

Her own kid.

Sure, I'd fucked up a few times, but that was part of growing up.

The violin screeched. It was my fault I'd used up all my lifelines. Time to accept the fact that I'd have to succeed—or fail—on my own. I could do this.

Ding-a-ling.

The bell caught my attention. I half turned my head, only to blink as I saw a familiar sign.

Same-day dry cleaning available. Please ask inside.

Holy fuck. It was the shop from my dream. A place I'd never been to before, yet I'd gotten all the details right, from the peeling paint on the door and window frame to the orange of the letters in the sign. Even the bell as I shoved open the door sounded the same.

As to *why* I went inside? Surely, the lady didn't—

"Fuck me, it's you!" I gasped as I saw her.

The woman from my dream narrowed her gaze on me. "Can I help you?"

"You were in my dream."

"How unfortunate for me. Was it a horror flick about the wrong choices my life could have taken?" She eyed me and pursed her lips.

"Uh. No." It occurred to me how crazy I sounded, barging in here and telling a random stranger that I'd dreamed about her.

"Did you need dry cleaning?"

"Yeah. But I can't afford it. I need a job."

"I would have said a shower is in order first because I doubt anyone will hire you smelling as you do." Her nose wrinkled.

"It's been a rough week."

"Excuses?" She arched a brow, and I was torn between shame and prickly anger.

Another person disparaging me. "I have the best one, seeing as how I died."

"And someone used Naloxone and brought you

back. Whoopee. The guy in the park does that a few times a week."

"I didn't overdose on drugs." Not this time. "It was alcohol. And I was clinically dead, at least according to the hospital. They thought I would have brain damage when I woke." Why did I feel the need to explain?

"Do you remember being dead?" she asked.

"I remember being judged." My lips turned down. "Apparently, I wasn't good enough for Heaven nor Hell."

"Did you see a lit tunnel? Or some shadow beasts?"

"Neither. Just some voice in my head getting annoyed with me. And then I woke up."

"You heard a voice," she repeated and then glared at her ceiling. I could have sworn she muttered, "Not what I asked for."

Definitely the lady in my dream. "Apparently, I keep disappointing everyone I meet. Join the club."

"What's your name?"

"What's yours?" I riposted.

To my surprise, she replied. "Sonja."

"Faye." A name I used to hate until I decided to own it.

"How did you find me, Faye?"

"I didn't. I was just walking when I came across this place. And it is weird, because, like I said, I swear I dreamed about it."

"Does that happen often?"

"What, dreaming?" I shrugged. "Maybe. I don't usually remember them when I wake up."

"Tell me more about this dying. You said there was a voice."

Sonja wasn't making fun of me, and for some reason, I wanted to tell her. "More like a presence. I understood it, kind of, even though it didn't actually talk."

"And what did it say?"

"The usual. How I'm a disappointment."

"Does that bother you?"

An odd question to ask, and one I didn't like answering. "Why would the opinion of others bother me?" I wished that were a lie, and yet, the truth was: I hated being judged. And I knew that was part of the reason behind my extreme behavior.

I came to that analysis from a course I took on human psychology my second year of college. I never took those classes any further because I didn't like what I saw in myself.

"What do you want out of life?" Sonja asked.

More weird querying. "I don't know. To have fun?"

"What about purpose?"

"What about it? Isn't the purpose of life to have fun and be happy?"

"*Are* you happy?"

Another weird question to ask. One I didn't quite know how to answer.

Ding-a-ling.

I turned to see who entered and scowled.

"You again?" It was my redheaded stalker, back with a misshapen nose and bad attitude intact. He didn't come alone. Two fellows flanked him.

"Yes, me. Your scent was easy to follow, witch," he lisped.

"I think the word you're looking for is *bitch*," I retorted, offended that I smelled so bad that he claimed to have tracked it. "I see, despite your previous lesson, you still don't understand the word *no*."

"You can see the Red Caps?" asked the dry-cleaning lady.

"Kind of hard to miss their ugly mugs, given they're right in front of me."

"They shouldn't be in here." The woman's eyes narrowed. "Get out."

At first, I thought she spoke to me, but then I realized that she stared past me to the creeper and his buddies.

"We will have her." Pretty sure the asshat meant me.

I shook my head. "You and your buddies can fuck right off."

"You are unclaimed. Fair game." He reached for me, and I danced out of reach, slipping around the counter.

"She is in my care," Sonja declared, which had me giving her serious side-eye. At the same time, I didn't refute it.

"Stay out of this, witch."

Apparently, dude held all women to the same low regard. "Listen, it's been nice catching up, but you and your buddies need to go before I call the cops." As if I'd ever call the boys in blue. The threat didn't scare them off.

Instead, they spread out, three against me and Sonja, who stood from her stool with a steely-eyed glint.

"You dare much," she declared. "Get out of my store."

"Your time is done, witch. Step aside, or it will end even sooner," Ugly declared.

"I'm not the one finished here." Sonja pulled a silver baton out from behind the counter. Skinny enough to almost be a needle. She waggled it in the air, and just as she aimed it, one of the guys dove over the counter at her.

She was on her own. The redheaded creep and the other fellow rushed me. I ducked and head-butted the closest one in the groin, then followed up with a left hook into his nut sac.

When I heard the high-pitched scream, I knew I had a few seconds to deal with the second. Only he grabbed me by the hair, pulling it and causing me to curse.

It hurt. Not to mention, made me mad.

Smoke tickled my nose, and then I saw the flames on the laces of his boots, a flickering dance that raced up his pants. My redheaded assailant released me and started yelling, slapping at his body.

He had worse things to worry about than me.

I whirled to see that the lady had her thug on the ground, wrapped in some kind of sticky web. As for the third, he visibly gulped.

Sonja cocked her head and pointed her stick. "Out. Now."

The smartest of the trio grabbed his sticky buddy and dragged him out the door, but the guy on fire, my personal creeper, fled deeper into the store, the flames having climbed his shirt.

That wouldn't end well.

I bit my lip. This would come back to bite me for sure. Especially once the cops got involved. Yet, technically, I'd not set him on fire. No lighter. No matches. Maybe there was camera footage that would exonerate me. I glanced at the corners of the room and saw nothing.

It occurred to me that I'd yet to hear him screaming. Surely, it hurt.

More smoke tickled my nose as it poured from the back room.

Sonja tugged my arm. "We should get outside. The fire is spreading."

Sure enough, the creeper's run through the back had lit the clothes on fire, and I imagined the chemicals would soon follow. And so, for the umpteenth time since my death, I watched something burn.

But this time, I actually felt bad about it.

8

"I'm sorry," I muttered to Sonja, knowing it was my fault that her business was about to burn to the ground.

"Apologize later. Let's get out of here." She grabbed her purse and tugged me through the door. We emerged to stand outside on the sidewalk, not alone as residents and shoppers came to watch the burning down of the dry cleaner—apparently not giving a shit about their lungs. Pretty sure the billowing smoke held more chemicals than even I cared to inhale.

It was only as the fire trucks arrived and began spraying that Sonja nudged me.

"No point in standing around. Come on, we'll go to my place."

We? "Are you sure you want to invite me?"

"There might be more to you than I first thought. Shall we?"

I might have asked more questions, but she was offering a place to go. My homeless ass could use a place to park it.

Turned out she lived only a few streets away in a brownstone, narrow but tall at two stories, plus what appeared to be a converted attic, judging by the curtains in the window.

"You live here alone?" I asked. We entered into a small vestibule, and I saw only one pair of boots and a single rain jacket on the strip of wood with its screwed-on hooks.

"You planning on robbing me if I say yes?"

"No." But I could understand why she'd ask. When doing crystal meth during high school, I wasn't always a nice person. Did my mom ever commend me for weaning myself off in time to graduate? Nope. She expressed surprise that I'd passed, and even more that I'd gotten into college.

When it came to learning, I somehow remained smart, and that usually got me lectures along the lines of: *If you just applied yourself, imagine what you could do.*

Have a boring life with a nine-to-five job in an office.

Not interested.

"I used to have a roommate, but she married and moved away," Sonja replied finally in answer to my initial query.

"Did she actually move, or did you kill her and bury her in your yard?" A joke that, only after it emerged, hit me as being in poor taste.

"The yard is paved over. It's where I park my car."

"You don't deny killing her?" I teased, trying to make my insult lighter.

But she remained serious. "I only kill my enemies. Don't become one, and you'll never end up in the basement."

I gaped.

She cracked a smile. "Relax. There is no basement."

It only eased my anxiety a little.

Sonja moved away, heading up a narrow hall. "Shall we have some tea?"

More like I should escape. Something wasn't right about this woman. Starting with the fact that I'd dreamed about her, but mostly because she shouldn't be inviting a random stranger to her place, especially not after what happened.

At the same time, if I left, I'd be back on the street. Hungry. Homeless. Smelly.

Did I mention hungry? Didn't tea come with scones or some kind of crap?

The hall led to the kitchen, the swinging door opening into a room with a black-and-white tile floor. While immaculate, it was like being transported back in time, the cupboards, painted white, the knobs, ornate and black. The counter held a hint of modern, being a dark granite, which contrasted with the island topped by a butcher block.

The kitchen table and its four chairs reminded me of the one my grandmother used to have, with metal legs and a linoleum-style top. The chairs had cushioned seats and backs, the vinyl a hideous floral pattern mix of yellow, orange, and green. The drapes matched, which was quite the accomplishment.

I sat gingerly, now wondering at my choice in following this odd lady home. Why had she invited me? She'd been skeptical of my whole dream, then interested in my death, and had yet to ask me about the creeper who'd followed me into her store. Not to mention, she had to blame me for it burning down. I chose not to think about the stalker possibly being dead, burned to a crisp by a fire I'd most likely started.

Yeah, me. Because one fire was a coincidence. Two, still not a big deal. But at a handful and counting with one thing in common, it became apparent that I had a fiery problem.

But how could I explain to Sonja that I hadn't done it on purpose nor knew how to control this weird power inside me?

Maybe the tea she served held poison or a drug. Could be she planned to knock me out to take her revenge. While she claimed no basement, I still glanced around for a door in case she lied.

My paranoia saw all kinds of possibilities, yet it didn't stop me from taking a sip of the tea—which didn't shoot back out of my mouth—and eating from the plate of cookies she set down.

All the cookies. And two cups of tea.

While she merely held hers and regarded me over the rim.

When I finished, she said, "How long have you been doing magic?"

9

THE QUESTION TOOK ME BY SURPRISE, AND I choked. The cookie bits in my mouth spewed, a rain of crumbs all over her clean kitchen.

I could admit I'd not expected her queries to start so directly, but the food had earned her some leeway. "If we're talking magic mushrooms, then I was fifteen or so my first time. Meth was seventeen." And short-lived. I preferred the more mellow high from hash and marijuana.

"I mean actual magic. The hocus-pocus kind." She waggled her fingers. "When did you first start doing it?"

"I can't do magic." Magic wasn't real. What I had was some pyrotechnic ability, like an *X-men* mutant.

Ooh, maybe I should give myself a cool name. I used to drink with a guy who'd called me Hot Tits.

"I am not stupid, child. You reek of it. Why do you think you caught the attention of the Red Caps?"

"That smell is called not showering because I've been traveling."

"Not that kind of smell," she said with a wave of her hand. "Magic. And don't deny it. I saw you call forth fire on the Red Cap leader."

My mouth rounded. "Wasn't me. I don't know how that happened." I wasn't about to admit that it had occurred a few times before.

"You definitely conjured it."

"That's crazy talk. People don't *conjure* fire." A thing I kept saying to myself. People also didn't see lizard men, one-eyed cyclopes or gremlins. Yet, that kept happening, too.

"If you still think that, then your powers must be relatively new."

"I don't know what you're talking about. Magic isn't real."

"Magic *is* real. The supernatural, as humans call it, exists."

Sonja was nuts. I eyed my tea. Hopefully, not the

drugging kind. "I don't know what you're talking about."

"Let's backtrack for a moment. In the store, you seemed to indicate that you'd previously met the Red Cap who entered."

"Only the tall redheaded dude. I caught him stalking me earlier, so I clocked him. Guess he didn't like it, hence why he came after me again with his friends."

"Your power attracted him. It oozes from you because you aren't shielding. Which I guess does lend credence to your claim of being new at this, or you'd never have survived this long. Power attracts the wrong sorts."

I snorted. "Hardly powerful. But I am a magnet for perverts, apparently."

"I wonder if he planned to keep you or hand you over to his master," she mused aloud.

"Wait, is he like a human trafficker?"

Rather than reply, she had a different question. "How did he appear to you?"

"Tall. Red-haired. Freaky smile." With a way of moving that gave me the heebie-jeebies.

"Interesting that you could see him in his true form."

"Not really since you saw him, too." Duh.

"Do people sometimes appear oddly to you?"

"Depends on your definition."

"People who don't seem...human."

The fact that she'd mentioned it had my heart stopping, only for me to sigh and say, "I'm dreaming again, aren't I? My subconscious is trying to make me think that seeing lizard men and other monsters is normal. It's not. But I appreciate the try."

"So, you *are* seeing past the veils, which isn't a common trait. You reek of magic. Perhaps I didn't cast the spell wrong," she mused aloud.

"What spell?"

She ignored that to say, "Other than seeing and calling fire, what else can you do?"

"Nothing. Because I'm a normal girl."

"A 'normal girl' wouldn't have a Red Cap after her or be led to me. Have you managed to create any charms, accidental or not?"

"Are you asking if I'm a witch?" I snorted. "I wish I were. I'd hex a few fucking people." Starting with my professor, who hadn't liked my term paper. He'd asked us to research a known evil killer of the masses and find a way to make them likeable.

Just like with my history assignment, I'd chosen Satan. My very Christian teacher wasn't happy that I praised the dark lord for twenty pages. I could have gone on even longer, but I had a kegger to attend.

"And once more, you prove how unsuitable you are for the task ahead." Sonja rolled her eyes and sighed.

For some reason, I felt a need to explain. "Sorry, but whatever your task is, I'm out. I've got enough shit on my plate as it is."

"You won't have a choice if the Fates say you're involved."

"Hell, yeah, I have a choice."

"And yet, here you are."

"I'm here because you invited me."

"You only found me because of the spell I cast."

Implying magic, which I didn't believe in. Fantasy and paranormal bits were for movies and books. I lived in the real, depressing, and oft-shitty world. "I found you because I was looking for a place to crash." I didn't mention following Polkie, my imaginary lizard.

"You came looking because we met in a dream."

"And we're in another dream right now. Which means, yummy as those cookies were, I haven't eaten. I'm going to be so hungry when I wake up." My lips turned down.

"This is reality, Faye."

"No, it's not. Because dreams aren't real."

She pinched me—hard enough I yelped and jumped from the chair.

"What the fuck?"

"Just proving my point so we can stop wasting time."

"I'm leaving."

"No, you're not. We both know you're meant to be here with me."

"Is this your way of asking me to be your roommate? If so, you should know I can't pay you."

"Who said anything about money?"

My eyes widened. "Listen, I know I've done things to get by before, but I'm not a whore for hire."

Sonja clucked her tongue. "Do you always jump to the worst scenarios?"

"In my experience, people don't offer things like room and board for free. You want something."

"Eventually, you will pay your fair share. But until you can afford to do so, my only expectation is that you follow a few rules of the house. Clean up after yourself. No stealing. No alcohol or drugs."

I might have handled the tidy part, and I'd already given up on most drugs, but booze? I might not have a taste for it now, but that wouldn't last. I loved my drink a little too much. "I'm out."

"What?"

I shook my head. "You're not my mom. You can't tell me what to do."

"Someone has to, especially since you were gifted this magic."

"I don't have magic."

"You do, and you don't know how to control it. Just look what happened at the store."

I remembered but believing I could conjure flames out of nothing remained hard. "Thanks for the cookies and tea. It's been cool. Hope you don't have any problems with your insurance and that you find what you're looking for."

Because it wasn't me.

To my surprise, unlike my mother, she said, "Come back when you're ready."

As if I'd voluntarily return to the crazy house.

I left.

I regretted it soon enough.

10

Three weeks later...

My fist hovered by Sonja's door, unable to knock because, once I did, I'd have to admit that I needed her help.

I'd tried being on my own, but I swore, since my near-death experience, everything had changed.

For one, I was sober. So sober that even thinking of drinking now made me nauseous. The reek of pot, once ambrosia to my senses, made me gag. It meant seeing the world—and myself—clearly and not having anything to blame for my runaway mouth or actions. Of interest, I wasn't as bold or rude while straight.

But it didn't help with my homeless situation.

A women's shelter did take me in and let me use their facilities. Even helped me find a job working behind a register at a fast-food place, which turned my stomach. Mostly because I saw how my favorite stuff was actually made. Pretty sure my imaginary purple gecko swimming in their fryer wasn't the least sanitary thing to happen in that vat.

I worked eight hours then hit the shelter for another shower to sluice off the grease from the deep-fat fryers. Dinner could be had at the soup kitchen serving meatloaf and sliced bread. Palatable with lots of ketchup. Polkie preferred it with hot sauce. *Don't judge me for feeding my imaginary pet.* At least, he had stuck around.

A week after arriving at the shelter, I tried hitting a bar, looking for a quick, no-strings-attached lay. I stuck to drinking soda, hunched over the sticky counter, the music too loud, the smells in the place repugnant. Polkie seemed to like it well enough, given he scuttled across the bartop, snatching stray peanuts.

The prospects weren't the greatest, but a horny girl shouldn't be picky. As expected, a dude eventually chose the stool beside me.

"Can I buy you a drink?"

I offered him a smile and said, "Just a Sprite for me."

His return smile had canines that didn't belong to a human mouth, and when I blinked, his shaven jaw turned hairy, as did his neck and hands.

What the fuck? When he said, "Want to go back to my place and make me howl?" I ran out of there, suddenly freaked. Was he not human? Or was it me?

I kept seeing stuff. Maybe I had brain damage. Perhaps the hospital had released me too quickly. It would explain why I thought the lady running the shelter had green hair and bark-like skin. Would a brain injury explain all the fires, too?

It had been happening more and more at random, usually in conjunction with me being angry. My manager at the restaurant, a pimply-faced teen, harangued me over taking too long to process clients and a deep fryer suddenly ignited, shutting us down for a few hours.

A hobo, claiming I smelled delicious, tried to grab me and yank me into an alley. The dumpster behind him lit, startling him enough that I pulled free.

But when I woke on the bottom bunk of my bed and saw my upper bunkmate, Sally—a lizard-headed woman—looming over me as if she'd like to eat my face, I had to admit that Sonja might be right. Because how else to explain why Sally's hair suddenly whooshed and turned to ash?

Rather than chomp on my nose, Sally screeched as she ran from my room. Before I got in trouble, I grabbed my things and fled. I thought about leaving town, only what would that accomplish? It was time to face facts. I had powers, and only one person appeared to have any answers.

I glanced down at my purple lizard. "What do you think? Should we tuck our tails and ask Sonja for help?"

Polkie appeared happy to trot ahead of me, leading the way, only to disappear the moment I stood in front of Sonja's door.

Sonja answered before I could knock. "Ready to be reasonable?" she said, not acting happy at all to see me.

"Could you be smugger?" I grumbled.

"This is annoyance and impatience that it took you this long to realize you needed my aid."

"I want to be normal again."

"You mean a drug-using drunk on a path to dying before she ever reached thirty?"

That stung. "Why do you care what I do?"

"I'd prefer not to, but it appears the city needs you."

I snorted. "The city needs me? That's a pretty broad and bold statement."

"It's the truth."

"Let's say it is. Why should I help it?"

"How about because it's the right thing to do?"

"Since you know me so well, you should know that I don't give a flying fuck about the right thing."

My head snapped as if smacked from behind. I whirled to find no one there.

"What the ever-loving hell?" I yelled.

"Watch your mouth or I'll do it again."

I turned back. "You hit me?" How was that possible?

She answered as if I'd spoken aloud. "It's possible because of magic, Faye. If you can tone down the whining and self-pity long enough to listen, I'll teach you how to use yours."

11

Me, doing magic? The world should tremble in fear. Or lock me up.

"Why do you want to teach me?" I asked as she stepped aside and let me into the house.

"For one, the city can't have you going around setting fires every time you get upset."

"I don't—"

Air smack. My head rocked as she flatly stated, "No lying."

I rubbed my noggin. "I might have had a few lapses."

"You need to learn control."

"Easy for you to say."

She whirled halfway up the hall to the kitchen.

"No, it won't be easy because you're not used to being in control of yourself."

"I like to party." I shrugged because I didn't have a great excuse for my behavior. I didn't come from a broken home. I wasn't abused or traumatized. Quite simply, I enjoyed getting wasted. At least, I used to. Dying really put a crimp in my ability to have fun.

"You don't need to be inebriated to enjoy yourself."

"How would you know? I'll bet your idea of a good time is making bat wing soup." Petty, and I expected another slap, only Sonja laughed.

"Shows how little you know about witches."

"I know enough," I insisted. "You brew potions, hex people, and dance naked around fires for the devil."

"You forgot to mention the orgies."

My eyes widened. "Wait, those actually happen?"

An enigmatic smile was my reply.

"How did you become a witch?" Had she died like me and returned?

"I was born with my power." I dropped my bag of stuff on the floor.

That caused a frown. "Pretty sure I wasn't, so where did mine come from?"

"Whatever deity you met when you died," was her answer, which left me gaping as she went through the swinging kitchen door.

It took me a moment to follow because I spent a second remembering that presence when I died.

I had so many questions. "God gave me magic?" being the first one.

"*A* god," she specified. "I'm not sure which yet. I prayed to the Earth Mother, and yet, your experience doesn't line up with the usual tales of her blessing."

"It didn't feel like a blessing," I muttered as I sat at the kitchen table, where a meal awaited us, along with two place settings—as if she'd been expecting me.

"Perhaps it was punishment." She shrugged as she handed me a bowl of mashed potatoes. There was gravy, too, and chicken, corn, even some hot rolls, which made me groan.

She let me eat, the food the tastiest I'd had in a long while. Only when I'd cleaned my plate did I lean back with a contented sigh.

"That was amazing."

"Good. Since I cooked, you get to clean up."

She walked out and left me with the pile of

dishes. I wanted to protest. Why should I clean? I was her guest.

Who'd come practically begging for help. And I was going to quibble over washing up? The woman had made me an excellent meal. I owed her something in return.

As I soaped, scrubbed, and rinsed, I had time to think about all the times I'd left my mother with a stack of crusty dishes. The friends I'd partied with and left before cleanup. The reflection made me realize how selfish I'd been.

I need to do better.

My mantra since I'd remained sober. More than a month, and in better news, the cravings were almost gone. Since meeting Sonja, and getting a job, I'd even stopped stealing, although I had no problem stuffing my pockets with any freebies I came across. Never knew when you might need a ketchup packet or some extra salt.

When the dishes were loaded onto the rack to dry and the table wiped down, I exited the kitchen to find Sonja in her living room, a narrow space with a couch, a rocking chair, and no television, but plenty of books.

A glance around had me asking, "Where do you keep your magic stuff?"

"In my workshop off my bedroom on the second floor. I keep everything there except for my wand." She held it up, a silver knitting needle, the same one she'd wielded in the store.

"That's how you do magic? Wave it around and...abracadabra?"

"It's not that simple. I have some protection spells stored inside it. It can also be used to draw new spells if needed."

"Do you also make potions?" Because the stories always showed witches with cauldrons and weird ingredients, like moss collected at midnight or unicorn horn shavings.

"Rarely. Most potions are in the realm of alchemy. Completely different field. A witch manipulates and wields her innate power through intricate patterns."

"Her?"

"Witches are female. Warlocks are male. But we both use magic the same way."

"Through patterns, you said. Only my fire just erupts when I'm upset without any mumbo-jumbo hand or wand-waving."

"Because it's an elemental magic."

Ever realize the more you discovered, the less you knew? "Meaning?"

"Meaning, you don't need to do anything but command it into being. Elemental magic is part of you. Spells, on the other hand, give shape and purpose to magic."

"When you say 'elemental,' you're talking fire, air, earth, and water." I knew those, at least.

"You forgot spirit. Which is rare, I will add."

"Do you control an element?"

"Air." Rather than smack me, my hair lifted as if caught in an invisible breeze.

"Cool."

"Very. If you're interested in knowing more about the fundamentals, I have some primers you can read." She held out a hand, and a book on the shelf floated to her. I admit to being envious, as that seemed like a much cooler ability than setting shit on fire.

I eyed the book and raised a brow at the title, *Sally Goes to School*. "That's a children's book."

"Look closer."

I stared, feeling dumb until the image on the book shifted, as did the title. Even the cardboard cover changed. *The Magic Opus*. I snared the book and flipped, realizing once I saw past the camouflage that the pages were old, and the text handwritten.

"This will give you a basic starting point when it comes to magic and the history of witches."

I used to love reading until I discovered booze and drugs. A part of me was so intrigued that I wanted to start right away, but Sonja had other plans.

"Put that aside for now, and let's start with your first lesson."

"Magic lesson?" I sputtered. "Shouldn't I know more first?" I waggled the tome.

"Textbooks are all well and good, but you'll learn more by actually doing magic."

"I've done magic," I muttered. It ended with the firefighters being busier than usual.

"Did you? So, you know how to call fire intentionally?"

"No."

"Have you even tried?" she asked pointedly.

"No. Because I was trying to be normal, and normal people don't set shit aflame."

"You're not normal, though, Faye. You're a witch, and the sooner you accept it and choose to learn, the better for everyone."

"Can't I get rid of it instead?" What if I didn't want to be a witch?

"Sure, just pray to the god that chose to save your

life, tell them you're ungrateful for their gift, and I'm sure they'll take it back."

The way she said it... "I'll die if I do."

"A god chose to save you and give you access to magic for a reason. If you reject it, then they'll take it and give it to someone else."

Harsh. It kind of left me no choice. "Where do we start?"

"Light that candle." She pointed to one sitting on the hearth of the dead fireplace.

I stared at the tall wick. Nothing happened. "Might be faster to use a lighter," I muttered.

"Or you could actually try doing as you're told."

"I thought the whole point of you teaching me was the fact that I don't have control over my magic."

"To achieve it, you must practice."

"To practice, don't I need to know what the fuck I'm doing?"

Smack. "Language."

I scowled. "Excuse me for being frustrated."

"I won't excuse you because this is what you do. The pattern of your life. Always giving up. Taking the easy way out."

"Oh, no, look at me, I'm human," I mocked.

Smack.

How did one dodge an invisible hand?

"I thought you wanted to learn," Sonja chided.

"The keyword being *learn*, not be abused."

She arched a brow. "Did that hurt?"

"No, but it *is* pissing me off."

"I don't care. Because you're irritating me with your juvenile attitude."

"If you don't like me, then why invite me to stay with you?"

"Because I want to help you even if you're rude."

"I'm rude?" My query pitched high. "I'm not the one smacking people."

"You're arguing with me."

"You don't hit people for having a lively discussion."

"You're deflecting so you don't have to try."

"Am not."

Smack. "Don't lie."

I began to seethe. "Stop. Hitting. Me."

"Then do as you're told. Light the candle."

"I can't."

"That's right. You can't. Give up without trying. You're good at that."

I clenched my fist. "Shut up."

"Or what?"

"Or—Or—" I clenched my fists and jaw, my anger boiling.

Which was when Sonja said softly, "Light it."

I wanted to tell her to fuck off, but I could feel the heat inside me, that spark, and before it could light the drapes or the carpet, I tried aiming it at the candle.

It lit, a giant column of fire. But it wasn't the only thing. The hearth ignited, too, the dry kindling stacked within erupting into flame.

I gaped.

Sonja nodded. "Strong emotions let you tap into it. We'll have to work on that, so you don't need to be angry to use it."

I eyed her suspiciously. "Wait, did you do all that on purpose to piss me off?"

Her sage smile said it all.

And despite myself, I couldn't help but admire her.

Maybe she *could* teach me.

12

With the fire lit, our lesson ended for the night.

"Grab your things, and let's get you settled in your room." Given the narrow size of the house, I expected a tiny spot, which would still be better than sleeping on the streets. I followed her from the main floor to the second, with its three doors, only one with a lock that glowed as I eyed it.

She pointed. "My bedroom, bathroom, and workshop."

So where was I sleeping?

We went up the angled steps, barely more than a ladder, to the attic. An open space with a window on either end, a brass bed covered in a quilt, a woodstove, and even a closed-off area with a compact bathroom.

"This is for me?" I whispered. It was more than I expected. More than I deserved.

"Yes. You'll find toiletries in the washroom, along with towels. Clothes in the dresser, although they might not be your usual style."

It was too much. "Why are you being so nice to me? I've been nothing but rude with you."

"You have, and yet, I'm choosing to see past your rough exterior to the potential within. You could do great things, Faye, if you chose."

"Me?" I laughed.

"Yes, you. You just need to have a little faith and accept that working hard isn't a punishment but a goal to a fulfilling life."

With those words, she left me, and I pondered their meaning. How was working hard supposed to fulfill me?

I still wondered as I fell asleep, the bed just right, until the first rays of dawn hit my face, along with a gecko's raspy tongue.

"Ugh." I grumbled as I rolled to stick my head under the pillow.

Too late. I was awake. I opened my eyes to see Polkie staring at me.

"About time you showed up. I could have used the moral support last night."

Polkie stared, unblinking.

"How'd you get inside?" A dumb thing to ask, given he was a figment of my imagination. Or so I assumed since no one else seemed to see him.

"How did you sleep?"

He cocked his head.

"Yeah, I slept good, too."

A tongue flicked. One I'd felt. I reached out to pet Polkie, the skin softer than expected. Was the gecko real? Given what Sonja had told me thus far, I truly had to wonder. Could it be my pet was real but invisible to most people?

Wait, was Polkie my familiar? Because witches had those, right? I'd have to ask.

The shower was tiny but amazing, the water hot, and after a quick scrub, I enjoyed it for a few minutes. In the shelter, we bathed on a timer to ensure that everyone could have a fair turn. This was luxury.

Exiting in a cloud of steam, I eyed my dirty clothes. I'd brought my bag up with me, and yet it appeared to have disappeared. Remembering what Sonja had said, I explored the drawers and found jeans, still with tags and no holes. T-shirts, plain ones without heavy metal bands or rude expressions. Cotton underwear. Socks. Even a cotton sports bra.

Eyeing myself in the mirror once I was dressed, I appeared ordinary, if I ignored the fact that I still had my piercings, bright pink hair, and a curled lip.

Heading downstairs, I found Sonja in the kitchen, making breakfast.

"Morning," I said.

"Hello. I hope you slept well."

"Great. Thanks." I slid into a chair. A moment later, Polkie perched on the table, tail almost wagging, which led to me clearing my throat. "Um, crazy question for you, but do you see a gecko?"

"What? I don't under—" She whirled with her spatula, and her eyes widened. "Oh. Hello there, little one."

Relief hit me hard. "So, I'm not imagining Polkie?"

"I assume you mean the purple lizard on my table. He's real, which I would have thought you'd have known. Have you not touched him?"

"Yes." I squirmed. "Thought I was going crazy because he felt real. Is he my familiar?"

Sonja laughed as she turned back to her cooking. "No. Witches, contrary to popular belief, don't have any."

"What is Polkie?"

"A gecko, by the looks of him." Sonja flipped the cooking pancakes.

"How do you know he's a boy? I wasn't sure."

"I just do. And he's a handsome fellow at that."

I swear Polkie preened at the praise.

"Why has he been following me around?"

"Because he likes you."

Well, fuck. I liked him, too. I gave him a soft rub on the top of his head, which got his back leg thumping, although he scooted the moment he saw Sonja heading to the table with breakfast.

A large plate of grub for me, a saucer with berries for him. I drizzled real maple syrup on my stack and dipped my bacon in it. A sweet and salty crunch that made me groan. I ignored the coffee in favor of the orange juice.

"This is amazing," I said when I finally leaned back and resisted an urge to pat my happy belly.

"A hearty breakfast is advised, given we have a busy morning ahead. Join me in the parlor once you're done with cleanup."

This time, my selfish and lazy side didn't grumble. Not after what she'd fed me. I'd gladly do the cleanup every day if I kept eating that well.

I hummed as I washed, even giggled a few times

as Polkie kept poking his nose into the suds and then sneezing.

Lizard uttering achoos? Funny as fuck. The act of washing had a calming effect on me, which, at the same time, rid me of the I'm-so-full-I-need-a-nap mood.

Once I'd drained the sink, I found myself ready and raring to go. Time for my next lesson. I thought I'd be setting shit on fire again.

Wrong. Today, Sonja chose to begin teaching me about patterns.

She started with the basic ones. "Circle is a protective thing. It controls what's within. It's why we recommend you practice casting inside of one." She pointed to the one on the floor.

Today, my lesson took place in her workshop, a room that appeared to belong to a forgetful professor, not a witch. The many things cluttering the space seemed at odds with the tidy floors below.

I pointed to the bookcase partially over the curve of the circle. "Doesn't that affect its ability to work?" I'd seen the movies. Circle of salt disrupted and kaboom.

"The circle creates a dome that affects magic, not physical items."

"So someone could step inside it? Say like a demon?"

She arched a brow. "Why would a demon be in this room?"

I shrugged. "I don't know. Because they want a secret artifact or something?" Again, my movie lore came in handy.

"Did you not read at all last night?"

I shrugged and didn't lie. "No. I kind of enjoyed the whole clean bed all by myself in a room thing."

She stared at me. "I'm glad. But tonight, while you're relaxing, try doing some reading to avoid wasting both our time with basic questions."

Irritation tried to rise in me. How dare she?

She dared because she wanted to help. I'd burned down her shop, and yet here she was, giving me a nice place to stay, food, and teaching.

I dipped my head. "Sorry. I promise to come better prepared the next time."

I got a curt nod in reply. The lesson continued, dumbed down I was quick to realize, to make up for the stuff I needed to know.

How to make a circle repel living things—*"Just in case something nasty does ever try to visit,"* said with a wink by Sonja. It involved a simple drawing anywhere in the circle. Apparently, it would add to the magic. Sonja sketched one quickly, which was when I realized the dark sections of the floor, untouched by any clutter, were chalkboard. Easy to draw, easy to erase.

She handed me the chunk of chalk. "Draw it."

"Me?" I'd seen it briefly.

"Yes, you."

"I'm not sure I remember what it looked like."

"It wasn't complicated."

Hand shaking a little, I inscribed it, the lines a bit wobbly, and the chalk darker in some spots.

"Not bad. Next time, try to do it in one looping scrawl." She wiped it clean.

I tried it again. Then she took a turn and pointed out where mine could improve. Once I could do it passably, we moved on to other symbols.

So many, my head spun.

And still, she kept going. "If you link this symbol with this one, you can heal. But cross it with this one, and you can harm."

"Can we stop for a second?"

"Finally, she is going to ask a question. Took you long enough."

I gaped. "I was being polite and not interrupting."

"How are you supposed to truly learn if you don't ask me anything?"

Fuck me. In doing what I thought was best, I'd messed up again. At least, I eventually caught on. "So, I get there's all these symbols and I gotta draw them right. But anyone can do this." I pointed to the slanted cross with a tiny circle at the vee of the straight slashes. "What makes them magic?"

"Ah, so you noticed they weren't active."

"If by *not active* you mean they don't seem to do anything."

"A symbol, as you noted, is just a drawing until you infuse it. That requires drawing on the magic around you, inside you, or maybe even in an object and thrusting it into your construct. As you do, you give it will. Purpose. Basically, a set of instructions that the pattern can handle."

"Just give it magic. Just like that." I glanced around then at my hands. "How?"

"That's a healing symbol. Place your hand on it and think of something on your body you'd like to fix. Nothing too big. Start small with a cut or a bruise."

"You make it sound easy." I grimaced but did as told, placing my palm on the chalked marks. Covering it. Thinking of how I'd like the zit on my chin to go away. Like seriously, I was in my twenties. I shouldn't have acne anymore.

I felt nothing.

Sonja spoke as if she heard me thinking. "Give it something to work with. Feel for the magic."

"What's it feel like?"

"You'll know when you touch it."

Eyes closed, hand flat, I sought within. *Hello, magic, are you in there?*

Nothing replied.

Would my power speak to me?

More like it ignored me. I kept my hand on the symbol, and nothing happened.

I opened my eyes and saw Polkie, sitting with his head cocked, watching me. "Hey, little guy."

As if happy I'd acknowledged him, he ran onto my hand, his body warming it. I appreciated the touch and smiled.

Then gasped. The palm of my hand heated, and then my chin tingled. My free hand reached to touch and found the painful lump gone. "I did it." My squeal sent Polkie scurrying.

It was the only spell that'd worked that morning. We spent the afternoon working on my fire skill. It refused to come unless I got mad. Only then did I manage to accomplish anything—and set every candle in her workshop afire.

Which led to her rebuking me.

"Control, Faye! Focus and channel it rather than letting it run wild. Or do you want to cause another Great Chicago Fire?"

"Wait, that blaze was caused by a witch?"

"Don't tell me you believed the story about the cow?" Sonja scoffed.

"How many other famous people are witches and warlocks?" I asked.

"More than I care to discuss right now. We're in the midst of a lesson."

Eyeing my lopsided chalk drawing, I didn't disagree.

"Let's halt the fire practice for one last lesson on offensive magic. There are many types a witch can wield, influenced by region and culture. The one you'll probably find most familiar is this one." She drew a large pentagram.

"Isn't a five-pointed star like this supposed to be a devil worship thing?"

She snorted. "Only because simpleminded people group all magic into one category. Satan is only one of the deities out there."

"Exactly how many are going around giving people power?"

"An exact number is unclear because their prevalence waxes and wanes depending on those who believe. The problem being that even deities only have finite magic to give."

"Still no clue on who gave me my powers?"

"The fire narrows it down."

"To?"

"Well, there is Brigit."

"Never heard of her."

"Belenus and Hestia."

I shook my head.

"While rare in these times, Satan does still sometimes choose a champion on Earth."

I blinked. "Me, Satan's handmaiden?" Had to admit, it might be kind of cool. Just imagine the outfits I could get away with.

"A possibility, and before you get all crazy about it, the Satan in the Bibles is very different from the actuality. Keep in mind that the depictions you see were planted by his jealous brother."

"God."

Sonja snorted. "A lofty title. His true name is Elyon. For a while in human history, he was strong.

Ruthless. And clever, given how, even centuries later, people still revile Satan."

"Are you telling me the devil is a nice deity?"

"Oh, no. Never. He is quite evil when he chooses, but all gods are to a certain extent. Keep in mind they don't view the world the same as we do. What we see as depraved, is entertainment for them."

That nugget and others filled my head, followed me into sleep, and kept me occupied as I learned more and more.

Such as that the star had five points for the five elements. Invoking those points would strengthen whatever offensive spell I cast.

A pentagram I could stand in was more effective than one drawn in the air. However, if in a stressful situation that required magic, guess which one I'd have to rely on.

Over the next few days, I crammed my head with information. Reading the book she'd given me and then discussing it over breakfast and during lessons.

On day three, I finally needed a break. Grabbing a jean jacket from the closet, I escaped for a walk, practically barreling out of the house.

At Sonja's shouted query, "Where are you

going?" I hollered back, "Period craving for licorice." Not entirely false. The odd part? I wanted the anise-flavored stuff and not the cherry for once.

"Don't forget to wear the charm."

Ah, yes, the charm bracelet. The patterns of protection woven of hair—*whose* hair Sonja wouldn't say—supposedly enchanted to hide my smell and magic from those with the ability to sniff out that kind of stuff because I'd yet to achieve a good personal shield.

The bracelet sat on my dresser, and my lazy—and hungry-for-licorice—ass was already out the door. No big deal. I didn't have far to go. The corner store was literally only a few blocks away. I'd been there twice already on errands for Sonja because witches couldn't conjure stuff out of nothing—which bummed me a little. How cool would it be to magic up candy whenever I wanted it? At least, I had a little bit of my last paycheck left, meaning I could buy my own treats.

Buy, not steal.

The door beeped as I entered, and I quickly found what I wanted and paid. As I gnawed on my stick of black licorice, the guy at the register yelled, "Miss, your change."

I glanced back as my free hand yanked on the

door and grinned. "Keep it." Twenty-five cents might not be much, but it felt good to tip for the first time.

Before I could face forward, I slammed into a dude's chest. Kind of my fault for walking out the door before looking, but still startling. I smacked into it, and just my luck, the brick wall didn't budge.

I bounced, falling backwards, and he did nothing to stop it!

13

I HIT THE FLOOR, LANDING HARD ON MY ASS AS I glared upwards. "Thanks a lot, asshole."

He arched a brow. "Is it my fault you weren't paying attention?"

"It's your fault I'm going to have bruises on my ass because you're built like a brick wall. Would it have killed you to grab me before I fell?"

"It is never okay to put hands on someone without permission." A snarky reply.

"Did you learn that in how-to-retrain-your-stalker class?" was my sour riposte.

His lips twitched. "Anger management, actually."

Staring at him, I was struck by his good looks. Tall, obviously, given how he loomed over me. Built solidly as my throbbing ass and face could attest. Add in chiseled cheeks, a square jaw, and sinfully dark hair swept back from his brow, and he appeared a mixture of ethnicities, the best of everything in one arrogant package that stepped past me without offering me a hand to get up.

Rude. I wanted to be mad, but dammit, how many rallies had I attended and gotten wasted at that chanted some slogan about how it was never okay to lay hands on someone? Personal space and non-threatening places were huge for my generation.

And yet, watching the older movies, seeing how men and women used to react, there was something kind of sexy about when a guy seduced. No careful wording to ensure clarity about a mutual encounter. Just unadulterated passion.

Did I want just any guy to manhandle me? No, but at the same time, I kind of wished I could evoke that kind of passion.

I remained on the floor as my non-chivalrous knight stepped past me, pack of smokes in hand.

I couldn't help but mutter, "With those kinds of manners, I bet you're popular with the ladies."

Before the door closed, I caught his gaze as he swiveled to eye me and drawled, "Very popular, actually. Care to find out why?" Then he dared to grin and wink.

Damned if he didn't have a dimple. The door shut, and he was gone.

I rose, dignity now more injured than my butt. In more positive news, I still clutched my licorice. I chomped it savagely as I stomped out of the store. Cloud cover had thickened since I'd walked over. It became dark enough that the solar-triggered streetlamps buzzed, the fluorescent bulbs a glare that did little to erase the pockets of shadow.

This part of the neighborhood had mostly residential buildings, the few shops on the ground floor boarded shut. Only the two restaurants appeared to have any signs of life.

I tugged a new piece of licorice free from the bag and began walking, feeling calmer with the candy in my mouth. Odd, that. As I chewed, I reflected on how my life had changed, and not just my taste buds. Something about walking alone invited introspection.

I had lots to ponder, starting with me being a witch who could wield magic, or at least I would be able to once I mastered the intricacies of it. Getting mad and setting shit on fire?

Easy-peasy. Setting a single tiny candle alight

without getting mad at the cake? I'd ruined dessert three times now.

As for the patterns and the magic? Those proved to be hit and miss.

Yet Sonja didn't give up. Even as I almost did.

"I suck at this," I'd grumbled.

"You going to quit already?"

"Why can't I do it consistently?" Yup, I whined like a little bitch.

"Because, of course, you thought you could learn to wield magic like this." She snapped her fingers.

I scowled. *"It's hard."*

"Of course, it is, or everyone would do it. Now stop your moaning and start over."

A tough teacher, but unlike many I'd had, she didn't cave to my petulance. It should be noted that my mother never had either. But with her, it was as if I couldn't help doing the opposite of what she wanted.

The difference with Sonja? For some reason, I wanted to impress her. Her praise made me glow.

Yet that wasn't the only thing pushing me. Honestly, the thought of being some kind of badass witch appealed like nothing else in my life ever had.

At the same time, I feared it because I didn't

understand. Why me? Surely, there were people better suited. Nicer, and more motivated, too.

I'd never been a team player or a giving person. What made the god who'd changed me so sure I'd use my power for good? A harsh analysis of my character, and yet true.

I'd been an asshole. Still was. Apparently, a girl couldn't lose a bad attitude overnight.

As I passed an alley, I glanced in and didn't react at seeing the kobold—the name for the green dumpster divers I kept seeing—sitting on the edge of a receptacle, going through a bag of trash. Sonja had explained that the things I saw, while unusual, were real. Although, obviously, not many could see like I could. You had to have a certain level of power to see through veiling glamours. In the case of the kobold, invisibility. The lizard men? They preferred to live amongst the humans using what Sonja called a glamour.

Though their name wasn't *lizard men*. They were Saurians. According to the chapter I'd read on their species, Saurians were intelligent and the most populous kind of Cryptozoid. Cryptozoid being the proper term for those who lived hidden from the world. Apparently, they frowned upon the term *monsters*.

Sonja had given me a book to help me identify the things I saw, which led to some giggling and incredulity because everything I'd ever been taught? All a lie.

The reality and truth included werewolves, vampires, mermaids, trolls, and even fairies. It seemed all the creatures of legend existed, although a few had gone extinct—unicorns topping the list on account of their magical horn. Other species, like Centaurs and sea kelpies, came close. Hence the heavy magical cloaking these days—something Sonja was partially responsible for.

"The Cryptozoids come to Urban Witches for glamour spells and other enchantments."

"Wouldn't the correct title be city witch?"

She'd shrugged. *"I'm not the one who came up with the term, but I can tell you the definition. An Urban Witch is tasked with caring for a region's population. Ensuring that its hidden citizens aren't seen. And aiding with any magical threats."*

"What about non-magical ones?"

"We rarely interfere with man-made matters."

"If you're called an Urban Witch, does that mean there are other kinds?"

"Yes. Aerie, Tremora, Laguna are just some of them."

I'd blinked. *"And each has a different job, I'm guessing?"*

"Correct. Although none as powerful or important as an Urban Witch."

"Can you tell what variety I am?"

"That remains to be seen."

I discovered more and more every day. Quite honestly, I enjoyed it. Something about my busy days and the learning involved fulfilled me. I barely thought any more about scoring some dope or conning some guys into buying me drinks.

I now spent my evenings in bed, reading the books Sonja loaned me and getting a great night's sleep. I had to admit, I enjoyed not waking up with a hangover.

Thud. Scuff.

I kept chewing on my licorice, even as I heard the steps shadowing me. Would the world ever be safe enough for a woman to walk alone at night?

I paused at a red light, choosing not to jaywalk despite the lack of traffic. My shadows chose to flank me, their lizard heads distinctive even through a side-eye. Despite Sonja's reassurance that the Saurians were mostly benign, they creeped me out in their human clothes with their forked tongues that constantly flicked.

"You are the witch's apprentice," stated the guy to my left.

I knew better than to talk to strangers.

"You will come with us," added his companion.

Rather than wait for a reply, they just each grabbed me by an elbow.

"Excuse me, but I don't think so." A tug against their grip showed they weren't about to just let me go. Sonja had warned me that I might be targeted.

"Are witches some kind of rare delicacy for the Cryptozoids or something?" I wasn't entirely joking, and neither was she when she said, *"Yes."*

Wondering if they were going to eat me filled my head as they lifted me and carted me toward a car.

Oh, hell no. First rule of being kidnapped: Don't get in the fucking car.

Before I could act, someone actually intervened.

To my shock, the brick wall I'd slammed into at the store punched the guy on my left, cutting his knuckles on his teeth. Not that he let the cut and streaming blood bother him. He laid another haymaker into the second guy.

To which they roared and attacked as one.

Now, I could have bolted given Brickwall had freed me. Chances were the Saurians would lose interest once they noted I'd fled.

Still, Brickwall had done a good thing, and I refused to pretend to be completely helpless. I reached for one lizard man, wrapping my fingers around his forearm as I thought of heat. Fire. Flame.

Nothing happened. I wasn't angry enough.

That changed when the arm I held flung outward, sending me flying. I hit the ground and skidded. Ouch. Shock burst out of me, and clothes ignited, not just those of the thug attacking me but also my wannabe hero.

He quickly stripped off his shirt, baring incredible abs, which led to me barely noticing my assailants taking off, clothes aflame yet not yelling.

I might have stared overlong. When Wall's gaze hit mine, he appeared less than impressed. In his defense, his irritation probably stemmed from the fact that his skin appeared red in spots, blistered from the fire.

One I'd caused but couldn't apologize for.

I bit my lip. *Say nothing*. Sonja had warned me about admitting what I could do to anyone. Most people would be like I had been. Skeptical. Let him think the flames a fluke.

Distract him. "What happened to your rule about not touching people?"

"Someone being attacked trumps it every time."

He took a step toward me and, with a quick reach, hauled me to my feet. No permission asked. Only male determination as he brought me to my tiptoes and growled, "Who are you?"

"Nobody."

"Don't give me that shit. What the fuck did you just do?"

"What do you mean?" I blinked my most innocent, which, given my piercings, I doubted he bought.

"The fire."

"Divine intervention." Said most fervently.

"Doubtful," was his disparaging reply.

"You don't think I'm angelic?" I batted my lashes as if they wanted to take flight.

"You might be many things, but innocent isn't one of them."

"And like the rest of the world, you'll judge me on my appearance rather than my character." Some days, I wondered why I didn't conform. Why I made life harder for myself.

"There's nothing wrong with your looks, and you know it." His gaze roved up and down, leaving me warm in places that shouldn't heat in public with a stranger. "Stay out of trouble."

"Make me." Said with a flirtatious smile because,

hello, this close, he had every single one of my erogenous zones tingling.

His nostrils flared as if he knew. His pupils dilated. I thought he might kiss me, but instead, he murmured, "You should learn how to control your magic before someone takes it from you." With that shocking statement, he left, a long-legged, lean stride that had me staring after his tight butt, the T-shirt he wore molding to his upper body, the ragged remains of his burned button-down dangling from his fist.

I'd lost control. Sonja would be pissed if she found out.

Would he tell anyone what'd happened? Who would believe him? And without a picture or video of me, did it matter? We'd never meet again.

I was so sure of it, but Fate decided to one-up that bitch Karma and had Brickwall in the living room at Sonja's home.

14

THE MOMENT I ENTERED; HIS GAZE NARROWED on me.

"We meet again," I mocked.

"What are you doing here? Did you follow me?"

To which, Sonja interjected. "I had a feeling you meant Faye when you told me what'd happened." Her glance turned into a glare for me. "Did you seriously let loose your fire in public?"

The woman who'd told me to tell no one, spoke about it in front of the stranger, which meant I could be honest. "Barely public. And for a good cause." I pointed. "I was helping him."

Being a true man, he snorted. "As if I needed any aid."

"It was two against one," I reminded.

"Bah, I could have handled more," he scoffed.

Sonja shook her head. "Both of you should have known better than to engage."

"I had no choice. Those two thugs grabbed me first."

"She speaks the truth about that," he grudgingly admitted. "The Saurian appeared intent on abducting."

"And, of course, you had to get involved." Sonja rolled her eyes. "You're just like your father, Anakin."

I snickered and was tempted to parody *Star Wars*. *Who was your father?*

"What so funny?" he grumbled.

"Your name. Anakin. As in Darth Vader before he went to the dark side?" I hummed the *Imperial March*.

"Aren't you hilarious? Do you really think I've never heard that before?" he riposted.

He called out my lame joke. It appeared I was off my sarcasm game. Blame being thrown for a loop.

"Why is *he* here?" I suddenly asked.

"None of your business, little witch."

"If you say so, little dick," I purred with utter sweetness.

The corner of his mouth lifted. "Is that supposed to be more comedy?"

"Are you always this conceited?"

"Are you always this annoying?"

"Children," Sonja interjected.

Anakin's jaw tensed. "You forget yourself."

"And so do you. Let us begin anew as if you've just met. Anakin, this is my apprentice, Faye. Faye, meet Anakin, a good friend of mine."

Was that code speak for ex-lover?

"Hey." I offered him a cool hello.

He ignored me to say, "You can't be serious. She's a little old to be an apprentice."

"And yet, this is what the Fates have given me."

"She lacks basic control," he grumbled.

"She's practicing."

He raked a hand through his hair. "Do we really have time for that?"

"We don't have a choice."

Cryptic conversations irritated me. "Are we done talking about me yet?"

"No." Him.

"Yes." Sonja.

Their opposing replies had me smirking. "Well, now that we've settled that, licorice anyone?"

15

No one wanted any, and given my company appeared to annoy Sonja's friend, I went to my room —the entire third floor attic thank you very much. More space than I'd ever had, and a haven to escape.

I'd finished the whole bag of licorice by the time Sonja knocked.

"Come in." She wouldn't come in without an invite. She had this thing about respecting my privacy.

"Anakin's gone, so you can stop hiding," she stated.

"Not hiding, just avoiding his annoying presence."

"I think you protest too much. We both know he's quite handsome."

"Holy crap, you guys hooked up."

She laughed. "Anakin and I were never intimate, but we have known each other a long time, which means we've reached a certain comfort level with each other."

"I don't have any friends." I blurted it and then could have bitten my tongue.

Rather than offer me a pity speech, or a things-will-get-better, Sonja gave it to me straight. "That would be because you were, as you'd say, an asshole. People don't want to be friends with people they can't count on."

I grimaced. "Your pep talks need work."

"I'm not here to lie to you or make you feel better. You know what you've done to alienate people, meaning you understand what you should do if you'd rather not."

"In other words, be nice and I'll make friends." I wanted to gag because it sounded so trite.

"Or don't. It's up to you. I have few by choice." She waved a hand.

"And Anakin made the cut?"

"You really dislike him? Why? I have to admit curiosity because women usually fall all over themselves for him."

"He's hot, don't get me wrong. I'd lick chocolate

syrup off him all day long, but his personality leaves a lot to be desired. Who knocks a girl down and then doesn't give her a hand up?"

"Anakin is very socially conscious and supportive of the feminist movement."

I wish I could say I wasn't. Yet I, to this day, remained a strong, independent woman. I did what I wanted. When I wanted.

That wasn't working out as well as I'd hoped, though. Some direction might not be a bad thing to have. Although, I would never get into the whole get-married, have-babies thing.

"He didn't stay long," I remarked.

"He had to get to his shop. He's short-staffed right now."

"Where does he work?" There weren't too many businesses open after dark in this part of town.

"He owns a pastry shop."

I blinked. "That walking hunk is a baker?"

"Yes."

"You're fucking with me."

"Why would I?"

"Because have you seen him? He looks more like he should be fixing choppers rather than icing cakes."

"How judgmental of you. And surprising. I

would have thought you'd know better than to be biased against someone because of how they choose to look."

"In my case, they were usually right." At least, they used to be. Rather than dwell on my shortcomings, I asked, "How come he's short on staff? Did they quit because of his shining personality?"

"More like Fate intervened. Margery went into premature labor and was put on bed rest for the last three months of her pregnancy. Nyomi decided to follow her boyfriend to New York. And with Leroy fighting with his partner, he's been calling in sick quite often."

"Looks like your friend needs to hire someone."

"He does, but not just anyone. Which is why I suggested you."

"Me?" I almost fell out of my bed. Sonja remained calm in the club chair she'd chosen to plant herself in as she dropped her bomb.

"Yes, you. You'll be working the night shift."

"What about our lessons?"

"You know the basics now. What's left is practice."

"How does me working in a pastry shop help me do that magic?"

"By giving you a purpose."

"Serving people treats isn't exactly a dream of mine."

"There's coffee, too."

"Be still my heart. I might die of excitement." Dry sarcasm, which Sonja ignored.

"Determined to hate it before you even try it. Typical."

"What's that supposed to mean?"

"You are perpetually convinced that everything and everyone is horrible. Annoying. Insert your paranoia of the day. The reality is, you're the barrier in your path to happiness."

"Me? Pretty sure I'm not screwing myself over." Spoken even as I knew it wasn't true. I'd fucked myself plenty of times.

"Fine, let's discuss the fact that you need a job. Because surely you didn't expect to live here free forever."

I'd not given it much thought since Sonja said she'd teach me to use magic. But I should have. What did Sonja get out of this relationship? A mooch who'd been rude to her friend.

It prompted me to say, "Sorry I wasn't nice to Anakin."

She snorted. "He's a big boy. He can handle it."

Then because I could be a big girl, I added, if a

little woodenly, "Thanks for finding me a job. When do I start?"

"Tomorrow night. Seven p.m. to three a.m."

"Okay."

I just prayed I didn't have to wear a stupid-looking uniform. But in positive news, I'd get to bug the shit out of Anakin and get paid to do it.

16

The pastry shop stood on its own with a parking lot encircling it. Only half of it was lit, and being street-smart, I stuck to those areas. Unlike most stores, the windows appeared blacked-out from the outside. I realized as I entered that they were one-way glass, meaning patrons could see out, but no one could peer in. The booths were nicer than expected, polished wood and brocade upholstery. The tables gleaming, the stain bringing out the whorls in the grain.

The counter stretched the length of the shop and appeared to be one impressive piece of granite. Most likely, it had a seam concealed somewhere. The stools were bolted down and of the industrial metal type that could swivel. The display case behind the counter held the expected racks of cupcakes and tarts, but not your run-of-the-mill variety. The flavors of a few boggled the mind, like jalapeno crunch topped with a cream cheese glaze, the pickle-flavored ones, the stuffed blood pudding variety. At least there were a few normal pastries like chocolate and honey-dipped.

The coffee machines were many and shiny, from regular carafe-style to intricate espresso-maker. A display case under the counter had bags of labeled beans, a scoop sticking out of each one.

It was just before seven, and the place wasn't busy, just some lady with the frizziest yellow hair I'd seen, sitting in the corner, reading a book with a giant mug by her hand.

A woman emerged from the back, hair straggling from her ponytail, her apron stained, expression harried.

"Welcome to Darkside Pastries. What can I get for you?"

"I'm Faye. I think your boss hired me."

"Think?"

"He's friends with my roommate, Sonja. She told me I was supposed to show up for a seven-to-three shift." Had she been mistaken? Was I about to embarrass myself?

"Boss said he'd take care of replacing Margery." She eyed me and frowned. "You have experience?"

"Eating treats and drinking coffee, yes. Making them..." I shrugged. "Does instant coffee count?"

"What can you do?"

Usually, I would have a smart-ass reply, such as *excels in sarcasm, great at taking breaks*; however, I needed this job, for more than a few reasons.

With that in mind, I toned down my usual asshattery to say, "Not much, but I learn quick." Not a real lie. I might learn slow with magic, but I usually excelled with other things.

"Better hope so. Because the nine p.m. Tuesday rush is no joke."

I almost laughed because it sounded absurd. But seeing her face, I held it in. She spoke seriously, and she'd not told me to take a hike.

"Hope I'm a help instead of a hindrance."

"I'm Leslie, by the way."

"Faye."

"As you can see, we're casual but clean for our uniforms." Leslie wore black molded jeans, a dark-patterned blouse tucked in, and cute little velvet boots. Her hair was loose, and her makeup subtle.

Me? I wore jeans with no holes and a plain T-shirt. It wouldn't be my clothes that people noticed.

Nor would anyone sniff my supposed magical scent, given Sonja made sure I wore my hairy bracelet, ignoring me when I claimed that the health department wouldn't like me having it around food.

"Where should I start?"

If I expected her to hand me a rag and tell me to clean. Wrong.

She said, "Follow me. First, we'll go over the kitchen."

Only as Leslie turned did I see the tail coming out the back. Long and fluffy at the end. It hypnotized me as it waved in the air.

I almost asked her what she was, only Sonja's lesson stopped me. *Never ask, wait to be told. Some species can be quickly insulted if you do.* Running through my mental catalogue, I did have a few theories about what she might be, kitsune at the top of that list.

The kitchen we entered appeared immaculate.

"Where's the chef?" I asked.

"Currently at home, sleeping off an ugly cry and a vat of double mint chip. But we should be okay. Armand, our morning cook, made extras. We've restricted the evening menu, given Leroy's absence."

"You don't bake?"

"That would be cruel to people's palates."

Ha, now that was an answer I could get behind.

She pointed. "Refrigerated specials are in there." She pointed to a metal door set beside a thermostat. "The ovens are always hot for those who like their pastries heated." It resembled a pizza-style oven and radiated heat.

"What's that door?" I asked, pointing to one with a keypad on it.

"Boss's office. No one goes inside but him. And don't let anyone bully you into breaking that rule. They are well aware that they can only get the sprinkle special via Anakin."

"Is that his signature dish?"

"For someone who's friends with our resident Urban Witch, you really know nothing, do you?" She shook her head. Why did I always get that reaction?

In good news, she was obviously Cryptozoid, which allowed me a certain level of honesty. "I'm new to the lifestyle." A basic way of admitting my ignorance to the world of magic.

She cocked her head. "You can't be that new given your age."

"So I've been told. And yet, only a few weeks ago, I was a flunking college student drinking her way to an early grave."

"Life-altering event caused you to get powers?"

Before I could answer, she nodded. "Rare, but it happens. Explains why Sonja sent you here."

"Explains it how? Because I don't get how working in a pastry shop is supposed to help me."

"You'll see. I wouldn't want to ruin the surprise." Her tail wavered and dipped close enough that I lifted my hand to brush it away.

Her eyes widened. "You see me."

"You're standing right there."

She glanced at her tail and then very deliberately aimed it at my face.

I ducked. "I'd rather you didn't."

"You can see my tail. That's a bit rare for your kind."

"Sonja wasn't surprised that I could."

"Because Sonja only deals in exceptional people."

Me, exceptional? I wanted to refute it, but I allowed myself to instead foster a spark of pleasure. Who doesn't dream of being special?

Over the next two hours, and very few clients, Leslie taught me the register and the names of the specials not on the wall. Many of them stomach-churning. It quickly became clear that the clientele of this bakery-slash-diner wouldn't be run-of-the-mill.

When the nine o'clock rush hit, I saw how right I was. A steady stream of clients began entering. Some appeared quite normal, no tails or lizard faces. Others were terrifying, and I served them wide-eyed and a little trembly, wondering if I'd end up being the one eaten.

My nervousness must have been noticeable. Leslie shook her head and muttered, "Cryptogin."

Only during the eleven o'clock lull could I ask her what she meant. "What's a cryptogin?"

"A mash-up up of Cryptozoid and a virgin. You are familiar with Cryptozoid, the term used for sentient non-homo sapiens?"

"Yeah, I recently learned it means anyone not human." Of which, there were more than I was comfortable with.

"There you go, making that face again." Her tone clearly said that I was being rude.

Usually, it wouldn't bother me, but I liked Leslie so far and felt a need to explain. "A month ago, witches and goblins and other creeps were only special effects on television or the big screen to me. Now, they're taking coffee, two sugars, one arsenic, and a squirt of toad venom." Which was cleverly labeled frog milk to fool any health inspectors. The fact that amphibians didn't lactate had apparently never occurred to anyone.

"And how has that discovery changed anything?"

I opened my mouth to explain, only to realize that, for her, this was normal. "It's shocking to realize there's an underworld to the one I used to see."

"I'll ask again, what changed?"

"I did," I blurted. And then really listened to what I admitted. I'd changed. Me. Nothing else. The world had always been like this.

It was then that Leslie pulled a Sonja and offered a blunt, "You do realize you're now a Cryptozoid, too."

"Me?" I shook my head. "My parents were human. I wasn't born this way."

"Earlier, when I asked about a traumatic event, you indicated yes."

"I got my power after I came back from the dead."

"Ah, so you're a Revenant Witch."

"A what?" I said with a frown.

Which was when Anakin chose to appear and say, "A zombie sorceress."

17

"I am not a zombie," I hotly declared, whirling on him. My heart raced at the sight of him, as handsome as I recalled. As smug, too.

"You died and came back to life. That's the exact definition of a zombie."

"Except I'm not rotting or craving brains." I knew my undead lore.

"Yet," he asserted.

"Ever." I'd become vegan before I started eating brains.

"You shouldn't make false declaration, especially since you've yet to try our Cerebral Delight." Only the dimple gave away that he teased.

"I'll give you a delight," I grumbled, clenching my fist, doing my best to not set him on fire.

"Someone just came in. I'll handle it." Leslie chose to leave us bickering in the kitchen.

It meant I was alone with Anakin in the vast cooking area, which suddenly seemed too private. Too small. "I should help her."

"Leslie's fine."

"I don't want her to think I'm slacking."

"Don't you mean you don't want *me* to think you're shirking your duties? I am, after all, the one who hires and fires."

"Are you going to fire me?" I hoped not. For one, I needed a job. And two, I didn't want to let Sonja down.

"Have you given me cause yet? I'll admit I am impressed that you actually showed up. I wasn't sure you would."

It hit me bluntly. "You didn't want to hire me, did you? Sonja made you."

"No one *makes* me do anything. I hired you because...why not? Worst-case scenario, you quit, or you're shitty enough that I fire you."

"Thanks for your vote of confidence. Well, here I am. So, suck it." Not exactly the smartest thing to say to my boss.

"For now. How long before you quit?"

"That's a dick thing to say. Unless you're planning to make it impossible for me to work here. What should I expect? Shitty hours? Sexual harassment?"

"You're too high-strung to last."

"High-strung?" I almost screeched then calmed myself into glaring. "I think I have a right to be a little freaked out, given my entire world has been fucked sideways."

"Get over it."

"Fuck you." The stove behind me ignited.

He eyed it. Then me. "Burn my place down, and you won't find me as nice as Sonja was about her dry-cleaning store."

"It was an accident. We were attacked."

"And you overreacted instead of dealing with it."

"How would you know? You weren't there."

"You forget I saw you in action last night."

"I'm trying to get better at controlling the fire thing," I mumbled.

"There is no *getting better*. It's your magic. Master it."

"Easy for you to say. You don't have my problem."

"I have my own burdens, but you don't hear me complaining."

"Well, la-dee-da for you. Must be nice to be so perfect."

His head turned sharply, and instead of replying to me, he said softly, "Wait here."

He left the kitchen, and I mostly listened, with my ear pressed to the swinging door, in time to hear.

"...your kind aren't welcome since the incident."

"Surely, that's water under the bridge."

"What do you want, Damian?" Anakin asked, his voice low and unimpressed.

"Rumor has it there's a new witch in town."

"No idea what you're talking about," drawled my new boss.

"Strange, given your friendship with Sonja. I hear she's taken on an apprentice with a fiery touch."

My blood ran cold. So much for keeping my secret. I wished the swinging door had a window for me to peek.

"Sonja's long overdue for some help, wouldn't you say?"

"Sonja should have retired a long time ago. What a shame about her last apprentice."

Wait, what? I almost went out to ask what he meant.

Anakin's voice lowered. "We both know you had something to do with that."

"Me? What did I do?" The low chuckle sent an army walking over my grave.

"Stay away from Sonja and her protégé."

"Or what? The time of reckoning approaches. Who will prevail?"

"Not you if I have anything to say about it."

"And yet, it won't be your battle to fight."

"Nor is it yours, even if you're pulling the strings." More cryptic talk.

"Jealous? Soon, this will be my city, and there's nothing you or Sonja can do to stop me."

There should have been ominous music to go with that statement.

Instead, I almost lost some teeth as the door to the kitchen hit me.

18

This time, I didn't land flat on my ass. Anakin grabbed hold of me as I ran my tongue over my teeth. Intact, but my nose throbbed a little.

"That door is a hazard," I grumbled.

"You know what they say about eavesdropping."

"You hear the juiciest gossip?"

He didn't appear amused. "I guess I should count myself lucky that you didn't come bursting out."

"I'm curious, not stupid. Who was that guy asking about me?"

"Damian."

"As in the evil kid whose daddy is Satan?" I joked.

He wasn't when he muttered, "Close."

I blinked. "'Scuse me?"

"Damian is demon spawn and not someone whose attention you want."

"Hold on a second. Do you mean demon as in horns and hooves?"

"You're thinking of a full-fledged demon. Spawn take after their human mothers on the outside."

"And on the inside?"

"They crave pain, blood, and death."

"Sounds lovely."

"They are also power-hungry, so the fact that Damian is aware of your existence means you'll have to be extra careful."

"You make it sound like he wants to kill me." Said on a laugh.

"I imagine what he has planned is worse."

"What could be worse?"

I never did get a reply, because the midnight rush kept us busy until two. Once it died down, my boss was nowhere to be found. Just Leslie and me, wiping down the tables and the counter. When I asked about mopping the floor and other deeper cleaning, she laughed.

"That's for the maintenance crew to handle."

Sweet! After a full day's work, I was tired. I'd gotten

used to being a daytime kind of girl. I couldn't wait to get to bed, even as I dreaded the walk back to Sonja's place. The twenty-minute jaunt seemed so long.

"See you tonight," Leslie chirped as I headed out the door. She planned to finish sending an inventory list before locking up.

How pussy of me was it to want to wait and see if she would be going in the same direction?

Don't be afraid. That Damian demon fellow had no idea I worked at the shop. I'd thus far handled all those who'd attacked me. I'd be just fine. I didn't need—

"Want a ride?"

I screamed, whirled, and only at the last second managed to not set my boss on fire.

And he knew it, too.

Anakin arched a brow. "Did you almost barbecue me?"

"Don't blame me for you popping out of nowhere and startling me."

"You should be more aware of your surroundings."

"I wasn't expecting to get accosted the moment I stepped outside. You know, it would help if the door had a window."

"Or you could pay attention. Now, do you want a ride or not?"

I should say no. But...my tired feet had other plans.

"Yes." I could admit, I expected him to drive something sexy and sleek. Maybe a sports car or a giant SUV. He had a basic-looking, four-door Kia sedan.

My expression must have shown my surprise because he snorted. "Expecting something else?"

"It doesn't seem like you."

"The price tag was half that of a luxury vehicle and the insurance a fraction."

"That's very practical of you."

"I'm a businessman. We always balance costs."

I slid into the front seat of his immaculate car. While not a luxury sedan, he had it fully loaded with leather seats, climate control, and a slick, upgraded sound system. As he pulled out of the parking lot, the sign for the store blinked off, and I had to ask, "Why a pastry shop?"

"Why not?"

How to say that he seemed more the type to own a motorcycle one?

He answered as if he'd read my mind. "Food

never goes out of style, especially when you offer delicacies no one else does."

"Your clientele is almost all Cryptozoid."

"Yup."

"But you're not one."

"Says who?"

I eyed him, hard, trying to see past any possible glamour, but he remained handsome as ever. No extra body parts. No second row of teeth. Perhaps his clothes were what made him special.

"What are you?" I finally asked.

"You don't really think I'm just going to tell you, do you?" He glanced at me only long enough to offer an enigmatic smile.

So, I blurted out the first thing that came to mind, given his luxurious head of hair. "Werewolf."

He laughed. "Are you just going to guess?"

"You didn't deny it," I prodded.

Rather than answer, the car slid to a stop, and he said, "Good night, little witch."

My walk might have held more sway than usual as I headed for the front door because I knew he watched.

He didn't drive away until I was inside with the door locked behind me. But he didn't go far. He spent the night in my dreams.

19

I was in bed and asleep by four a.m. and up at noon on the nose. Eight hours. Decent, and I felt pretty good, considering.

Over that next week, I fell into a routine. It involved magic practice in the afternoon—where I finally learned how to light a single candle *and* snuff it. A bit of drawing and infusing. I'd gotten good at the healing and got rid of some scars that embarrassed me now.

After my shower, I had dinner with Sonja then headed off to work—but not on foot after day two. By starting an hour earlier, Leslie could swing by and grab me. She drove me home most nights, too. Dare I say we were becoming friends?

I rarely saw my boss, and when I did, sparks flew. The man knew how to piss me off quickly, but after that first lapse with the stove, I kept my fire under control—and I could have sworn I saw approval in his gaze—along with smoldering interest. An interest he kept to himself.

He never did anything untoward. Treated me the same as he treated Leslie. Tell that to my dreams he featured in. He might not have tried to seduce me, yet part of me wanted him to. Especially since he fueled my masturbation daydreams.

Yes, he featured in my fantasies, even as I recognized that we would never actually fuck. He was my boss, and I needed the job, and not just because of the paycheck. I didn't want to let Sonja down. She'd been there for me when I hit rock bottom. Believed in me even as she didn't put up with any bullshit. Add in the fact that I liked Leslie and even the patrons I was beginning to know, and I was happy.

Happy enough that during my two days off, I missed going in to work.

Huh. I didn't think that had ever happened before.

I spent my weekend—consisting of Monday and Tuesday—practicing my magic. Reading. Getting more licorice but not running into any fleshy brick walls.

Maybe my luck would change at the shop tonight.

As part of my new schedule for work, I woke at noon and found the house empty. A plate of food in the fridge had been left for me to nuke, along with a note from Sonja. *Running errands and will miss our lessons. I left a book out for you to read if you'd rather not spell alone.*

Given the worst I'd done to myself was turn my hair a hideous, normal brown, and another time an electrical zap, I didn't worry too much.

I hit the workroom with its giant circle with a plan to work on a portable shielding spell. Since I'd mastered doing it in chalk, it was time to progress to other methods, such as wand-waving like Sonja did. I even had a slender finger of birch, a beginner wand she'd declared as she gifted it to me a few days ago.

I'd yet to ask why we couldn't just use a finger. Wouldn't it air-draw just as well?

The muffled sound of the doorbell had me pausing in my failed attempts to air-draw the correct pattern. How did I know I failed? My protective shield zapped me and left me with curled ends on my hair. I'd have to straighten it before work.

Heading downstairs, I didn't fling open the door. For one, not my house. Two, women didn't just answer to anyone. And three, I didn't expect anyone. Leslie wasn't due for another two hours, and Sonja had a key.

Beyond the filmy curtain covering the window in the door, I saw someone wide standing on the stoop wearing a long coat. When he turned, I saw the very masculine features replete with scruffy jaw on a human face. No lizard features or anything weird. Even if I squinted.

The man spotted me and waited.

I still didn't fling open the door in welcome. Instead, I cocked my head and yelled, "Can I help you?"

"I have a message for Sonja."

"She's not here right now."

"Who are you?"

"The maid." As if I'd say anything else.

"Maid?" I heard the skepticism, even through the door.

Which was why I chose to be a little smart-assed about it. "Yes, maid. Do you have a problem with my chosen profession? I'll have you know it takes a certain kind of person to get on her hands and knees to scrub toilets and tile."

"You look like the type who'd know about kneeling."

The rude remark offended. Before I could think twice, I opened the door to glare. "Listen here, asshole. The only people who are allowed to insult me are my parents, Sonja, and my boss. So, you and your little dick can fuck off."

"Do you know who I am?"

"Apparently, not. Nor do I care. So, why don't you take your attitude and take it for a nice long walk? Preferably off a cliff."

Coldness radiated from him to the point I debated grabbing a sweater. "I am an emissary for the Pantheon."

"The who?" I'd heard the term and scrambled to remember what it meant.

"The Pantheon. Those who govern all, even impertinent witches."

"We live in the United States, buddy. As a citizen, I follow the president and Congress's laws."

"You are a witch, and as such, you obey the Pantheon's edicts—or else."

I rolled my eyes. "Do no magic. Show no magic. Blah. Blah. Yeah. Yeah, I know. Sonja told me the rules."

"Did she also tell you that the time of the Choosing fast approaches?"

"The what?"

A smirk tugged at the corner of his mouth. "I see you're not as knowledgeable as you boast."

"And you're just plain annoying. So buh-bye." I stepped back into the house, about to slam the door, which was when the dude got freaky.

His eyes rolled back in his head until only the whites remained, and his mouth opened wider than it should. A chill emanated from him as a voice, not his own, emerged.

"Child of fire, born in death, face the truth and vanquish or forever be damned."

My scared butt just had to retort. "Tried the damning thing, but the devil didn't want me."

The dude kept going. "The Choosing no longer plods but sprints. The time is here. The time is now. Who shall be the last witch standing?"

"Sonja, because she kicks ass."

The guy's face snapped back to normal as he said, "This battle isn't hers. And given what I've seen of you, it would seem her goddess has forsaken her."

"Fuck you." It was one thing for the people I'd screwed over to insult me, quite another for a stranger.

"You're not my type." With that, he literally turned into smoke and disappeared.

As for me? Yeah, I shook.

My unease lasted until Sonja arrived. The moment she walked in, I blurted out, "What's the Choosing?"

20

Rather than answer, she had a question of her own. "Where did you hear that term?"

"Some dude came here looking for you."

"And you answered?" The sharp rebuke almost had me hanging my head until I remembered that I was a fucking adult.

"When someone knocks, you answer. It's called manners."

"It was dangerous. I have many enemies, and as my apprentice, so do you."

"Yet you let me walk to the store."

"Public places are mostly safe. And so is my house, if you don't open the door to the wrong sorts!"

"Sorry, I didn't know that. In my defense,

whoever it was knew you by name, so I assumed it was an acquaintance of yours."

"I'm the city's Urban Witch. Everyone knows my name." The tone called me dumb.

"Nothing happened. And you're deflecting. What does the Choosing mean?"

She turned from me. "Nothing you need to worry about for a while."

"Wait a second, what's that supposed to mean?"

"You'll find out when the time is right."

"How about now since it concerns me? Dude made it sound pretty important."

"It is important. You'll learn about it in due course."

"I hate secrets," I mumbled.

"It's not a secret, more just that you don't need certain things clogging up your brain space quite yet. Now, shouldn't you be readying for work?"

Meaning the conversation was over. But I couldn't forget it. I'd not seen that term in any of my books. I would have remembered. I'd not mentioned to Sonja that the guy had indicated it would happen soon. Sonja sounded pretty sure we'd have time to deal with it.

I hoped she was right, even as it continued to bug me.

Hence, why I asked my new coworker Leslie when I got to work, "What's the Choosing?"

Her eyes widened. "You don't know?"

Not wanting to lie, I admitted, "Sonja wouldn't say."

"Then neither should I." Leslie shook her head.

"Why not? If it's important—"

"It is very important, and I'm sure, when the time is right, she will teach you about it."

"That's bullshit," I huffed.

"What's bullshit?" Anakin asked.

My boss emerged from his office, and I glared. "The Choosing."

His response? An arched brow. "I'm surprised Sonja mentioned it so soon. I'd gotten the impression that she wanted you to be more trained before tackling it."

"She didn't tell me. Some guy who came looking for her did."

His expression sharpened. "Who?"

I shrugged. "No idea. He said something about working for the Pantheon."

Anakin's lips pressed into a line. "I see. I need to go out for a moment. If anyone asks for the special, tell them to come back later."

"Where are you going?" I asked.

"Out." He left abruptly, and I eyed Leslie.

"Was it something I said?"

"We should get ready. It's a full moon tonight, and I expect we'll be busy."

We were. Crazy busy with people I'd never met, who seemed normal at first glance, but when I looked at them a certain way, I caught an animal shine in their eyes. And when they got rowdy, they sometimes erupted into howling.

"Are those werewolves?" I muttered to Leslie as we sold out of our last bison-and-peanut-butter stuffed puff pastry.

"We prefer the term Lycan," a grizzled fellow stated as he approached the counter.

"Hi," I offered meekly. "Welcome to Darkside Pastries. How may I serve you?"

Rather than reply, he eyed me up and down. "I can see why the odds don't favor you."

I stiffened. "Excuse me? Do you have a fucking problem with how I look?" Yeah, my language could have used work, but the dude didn't appear offended. Just like he didn't appear impressed.

"I know better than to judge a person by their skin. That tells me all I need to know." He pointed to my hair bracelet.

"It's for protection."

"Because you're weak," he sneered. "A real witch doesn't have need of a charm to do magic. Pity what happened to Sonja's last apprentice. Now there was a girl who would have done us proud."

"Excuse me for being me," I snapped. "Since you're just in the mood to insult me, I have better things to do. Like watch the icing harden in the kitchen." I whirled and slammed into the kitchen, causing Leroy to cast me a dark look.

I flashed him the finger. I'd learned early on that the gruff man preferred my attitude to apology.

"What's got your panties in a twist?" he muttered, turning back to his creation of some cake that involved layers of meat and some slime that made me want to barf but had Polkie perched nearby, watching with big eyes. He knew Leroy was good for scraps and belly rubs. Probably why he showed up almost every shift.

"Werewolf out front. Says I'm a shitty replacement for Sonja's last apprentice."

"I wouldn't say shitty. Just different."

"Different how? Did you know her?" I couldn't help but ask.

"I did."

"And?"

"Yolanthe was a gentle creature. Kind. Sweet. Giving."

Not a claim that could be applied to me. "What happened to her?"

"She chose a different path than the one Sonja had for her."

"Is she dead?" I asked bluntly.

"Physically, no, but she isn't the girl she was. And never will be again."

I rolled my eyes. "Don't tell me you're going to give me half-assed answers, too, now. What happened to not being a bullshitter?" I'd met Leroy on day two at the store. He was gruff, blunt, honest, and accepting. He treated me like everyone else—with a lack of respect.

"People change. Some for the better." He eyed me quickly. "Some not." He glanced down at his almost-finished masterpiece.

"Does she still live in the city?"

"Yes. I imagine you'll be meeting her soon enough."

Leslie entered the kitchen, blowing bangs from her face. "I hate the full moon. I swear, if another one of those fleabags tries to slap my ass, I will lose my temper!" Angry Leslie was like watching a squirrel get pissed. Still cute and hard to take seriously.

"I'll go handle them for a bit. Why don't you take a break?"

"You sure?"

"If any of them try to get cute, I'll singe their fur." Because I could do that now without scorching skin. I'd been practicing. We'd see how mouthy they were without eyebrows or eyelashes.

It took me making the boldest one, with shoulder-length locks, bald before they finally eyed me with respect. Which was when Polkie chose to park his gecko butt on the counter, smirking, I swear, because the first guy that eyed my purple pet and licked his lips lost his luxurious mustache.

Eventually, the rowdy Lycans vacated the shop, leaving the place empty. We neared closing, meaning a round of tidying up. I'd just finished filling the salt and brimstone shakers when the door opened. My attention snapped right to it as a wave of something—I didn't know what to call it other than cold—sent a chill down my spine.

A beautiful man entered, the kind you saw on billboards with low-hanging jeans, partially buttoned shirts, and a square jaw advertising some kind of sexy cologne. His blond hair hung in waves just past his chin, but there was nothing effeminate about it.

He oozed masculinity. Sex appeal. And darkness. It clung to him like a miasma that had Polkie hissing before scuttling out of sight.

I wanted to join him in hiding, but while I might lack many redeeming qualities, I wasn't a coward. Not to mention, I was safe here. Leroy and Leslie were in the kitchen if I needed help. I lifted my chin.

"Evening, sir, and welcome to Darkside Pastries."

The man eyed me, and every inch of me crawled with repugnance.

"Go out back. I've got this." Anakin, who I didn't know had returned, suddenly appeared and nudged me to move.

"It's okay, boss, this is my job. I'm sure you've got more important things to do." After all, he'd not offered me a single ride since that first night. Not that I needed one. Or him.

"I said go." His voice was low and intent.

"Chasing her off before introductions, how rude." The beautiful man glided to a stop in front of the counter, meaning I got an up-close glimpse of his perfection.

"What do you want, Damian?"

Wait, *this* was the demon spawn from the night

I'd started? I'd not recognized the voice. More worrisome, it was the guy interested in Sonja's apprentice.

Me.

Before I could hightail it to the back, his gaze turned on me, and he smiled. "Hello, there. I don't believe we've met."

"Hi, I'm Faye." I blurted out the words before I could stop them.

"Faye. Such a lovely name for a lovely lady."

Me, lovely? For some reason, that word had a dampening effect on his charm. "What can I get for you?" I asked, pretending Anakin wasn't standing right there, glowering.

"You."

I blinked. "Me? I'm not on the menu."

"You should be. I can see why Anakin hired you. Even though you try to conceal it with your paltry charm, you smell delicious. Doesn't she?" A query directed at my boss.

"Leave my staff alone. You know the rules of my shop."

"Eat the wares, not the waitress. Pity. I'd have paid top dollar for a bite."

A freaky thing to say, especially once I saw his pronounced canines. Did half-demons eat people? "You heard my boss. No eating me." A rule that didn't apply to my boss. He could nibble on my parts anytime.

"You say that like it's a bad thing. I assure you, it's quite pleasurable," Damian purred.

"Says you. Pretty sure I wouldn't enjoy having chunks bitten out of me."

"What do you want?" Anakin snapped.

"You know what I want." His gaze slewed to me, and I shivered once more.

"Leave Faye alone."

"I will, but only because it appears she's not the threat I expected."

"Yet," Anakin growled.

What? For once, I listened rather than getting involved.

"Ever," was Damian's smug reply. "Perhaps if Sonja had longer to train, this morsel might have been a force to be reckoned with..."

"Still plenty of time for Faye to learn what she needs to."

"Is there? Because I've heard otherwise," Damian retorted.

"What are you talking about?" Anakin growled.

"Haven't you heard the news?" Damian said in mock query. "Sonja has been called to serve as emissary to the Pantheon, effective immediately."

21

Wait a second. What did Damian mean when he said that Sonja had been called to serve the Pantheon.

"Is Sonja leaving?" I might have sounded a tad pathetic saying it.

Anakin butted in first. "Impossible. Heztor isn't due to retire for a while yet."

"Unfortunately, it is Aellia who suffered a mishap and is no longer able to fulfill her duties."

"You lie."

The smirk on Damian's face would have made the happiest child cry. "Why lie when the truth is much more delicious?"

"You have something to do with Aellia having to step down, don't you?" Anakin accused.

"Me?" Damian once more mocked. "Would I do such a thing?"

"Yes, you would because you knew Sonja's successor wasn't ready."

"Ready for what?" I asked.

"You'll see soon enough," Damian stated. "Pity you won't survive. What a waste of tasty meat."

"Get out." Anakin's demand emerged low.

"Does the truth hurt?"

"You're just trying to unnerve Faye."

While I said nothing aloud, I wouldn't deny Anakin had it correct

"Admit it, she is nothing like Yolanthe. Weak. Unfocused. Untrained. This might be the shortest ceremony we've ever had."

"OUT!" Anakin roared, loud enough that the building shook. Well, shit. That was cool.

"I will since I see I've hit a nerve. Fear not, I've no plans to shut down your shop once I'm in charge. After all, you do make the best blood pudding." With that parting remark, Damian left.

But his threat remained, as did my glowering boss.

"In my office. Now."

I followed him into the kitchen where Leslie was

finishing sealing some leftover treats. She eyed us and frowned. "What's wrong?"

"Sonja's been called to serve the Pantheon."

Her eyes widened and turned on me. "Oh. I'm so sorry."

"What's that supposed to mean?" I retorted.

"Don't get pissy with Leslie," Anakin snapped.

"I wouldn't get pissy if people would explain what the fuck is going on," my pissy self snapped.

"Not here. In my office." Anakin entered the codes on the lock for the door. It beeped before opening. He swept an arm, meaning I got to go in first.

But once the door closed and it locked, I had a moment to wonder if I'd made a mistake. Because now, I was alone with Anakin, a man I'd mentally undressed.

A guy who blew more cold than hot. *If only he'd blow me...*

While I glanced around, my boss threw himself behind a desk and poured himself a drink from a decanter. The office was sizeable, probably at least a dozen feet across and closer to twenty long. The desk was the biggest piece of furniture, a massive thing made of carved wood with an ink blotter on top, a computer angled on a corner.

The far end of his office was a series of cabinets

with dial locks, inset with gauges. The walls held art, the abstract kind that I didn't understand.

What was the point of a painting that appeared as if a kid flung paint across a canvas?

"Sit." He pointed to a club chair, one of two dark red leather ones across from his desk.

I perched on it and opened my mouth, only to have him say, "Not yet." He pulled out his phone and began typing, fast and furiously, the replies arriving in short angry buzzes—actually, the angry was him.

When he finally slapped his cellphone on the desk, I was ready and managed a frosty, "Done ignoring me?" I'd have left if I'd not looked like an idiot trying to open the locked door.

"Don't get an attitude with me. I was verifying what Damian said."

"And?"

"True." For some reason, this agitated him, and he drummed his fingers.

"Care to explain what's going on?"

"Sonja has to leave."

"Because of this Aellia who had to retire?"

"Yes."

"How long will she be gone?"

"Forever."

"Oh." There went my new home and my apprenticeship. My shoulders slumped. "Guess I need to start apartment hunting, then." A depressing thought. I'd finally been getting my life together.

"No need. You can stay in the house." He waved a hand.

"Really?" What a relief because surely Sonja's rent would be reasonable. "Good to know. So, I guess the next question is, why are you freaking? I mean, isn't Sonja working for this Pantheon a promotion of some kind?"

"It is. But it leaves the city in a bad position. We need an Urban Witch."

"And I'm not ready." Spoken dully, even as I flushed hot. It humiliated to know that no one thought me capable. Hell, I knew I wasn't a proper witch, not like Sonja. But I'd been trying. Learning. It sucked I wouldn't have the chance to take over from her like she'd intended.

"You asked earlier about the Choosing."

"The thing that no one will speak about," I mocked with a roll of my eyes.

"Because we thought we'd have more time. Alas, with Sonja's departure, that clock has run out. The Choosing is a ritual whereupon the next Urban

Witch is selected. You were supposed to be the one to take her place."

I stiffened. "It's not my fault she got promoted early. I guess she'll have to call her coven or something to find a replacement."

"It doesn't work like that."

"Then how does it work? And no more of these half-assed answers or need-to-know bullshit. You're acting like it's the worst thing to ever happen."

"Because it is. There's no way you'll succeed in the Choosing."

"No shit. Which is why I said she should call in a pinch hitter."

"She can't. You are her apprentice. The one her goddess chose to take her place."

"What if I don't want the job?"

"It's not a question of want. You'll be tested."

"And if I fail?"

"You'll die."

Well, that wasn't cool. "I'd rather not. Find another witch." It actually burned me to say that because I'd begun to believe in myself. To look at Sonja and want what she had. Do what she could. To be a better version of me.

"The only other witch that is planning to vie for the position would be terrible for this city."

"Wait, there's someone else?" I blinked.

"You asked about Sonja's last apprentice?"

How did he know? I nodded. "Leroy says she was pretty much perfect."

Anakin grimaced. "Hardly perfect, given she succumbed to Damian's charm the moment he plied it in her direction."

"He seduced her? Ew." The man was pretty, but the stench of evil coming off him was a total turn-off.

"Seduced and stole her from Sonja. He saw the potential in her and decided to bend her to his will."

"Why?"

"Power, of course. As Sonja's former apprentice, Yolanthe is allowed to compete. If she succeeds in the Choosing, she becomes the city's Urban Witch. Only she won't be an impartial one like Sonja, given her ties to the demon spawn."

"I guess that would be bad for the city." I frowned. "Surely, there's someone else suitable to challenge her."

"No. Why do you think Sonja cast that spell, looking for a new apprentice? She went to great measures to find you."

"Wow, what a disappointment. Guess she was right when she said that she cast the spell wrong." My lips turned down. And, funny enough, I ducked, expecting the usual air slap from Sonja, only it was Anakin in front of me.

Glaring.

"I didn't take you for a coward."

"Everyone keeps telling me I'm not ready and useless." I flung my hands.

"No, *you* keep saying it. I'd hoped you'd have more training, but ultimately, the Choosing isn't about the spells you know or the patterns you can draw."

"Then what is it about?"

"Being the most suited for the task. And before you ask, I don't know what the criteria for that is. Meaning, we must prepare you as broadly as possible in hopes you'll pass."

"I'm not ready," I reiterated. "I need more time. More lessons."

"We'll have to work fast and hard."

"Since when are we a *we*?"

"Since the fate of the city lies in the balance. You'll need my help if you want to survive the trials. Damian will do his best to sabotage so Yolanthe can easily win. And we can't allow that. We need a strong Urban Witch to stand against his depravities."

"I take it Sonja's been keeping him in line?"

"Him and every other Cryptozoid. The magic

she uses to protect the city keeps all of them from being the monsters that humans fear. Once she leaves, those spells will start to fade, which is why a new Urban Witch needs to be chosen, so she might take over those spells before it's too late."

"Sounds like a tough job. I don't know if I can do it." I said it even as I didn't entirely mean it. Something about the idea of being someone held in high regard like Sonja was provocative. To be someone important, with purpose.

"Giving up already?" His lip curled.

"No. But let's face facts. I'm barely a witch. How am I supposed to help an entire city when I've only just begun taking care of myself?"

"Perhaps by having a little faith."

"You said I'd die if I failed."

"You've faced death before and survived."

I blinked. "By fluke."

"Try fate. Do you really think you're here by accident?"

"I think..." I eyed his decanter, wanting a drink, knowing I'd only spit it out. "I think I need to go to bed and sleep on it."

22

THE END OF MY SHIFT AND CLEANUP PASSED IN A blur. Leslie apologized for needing to stay a bit later to do inventory.

A poor excuse, meaning I wasn't surprised to find Anakin outside waiting for me.

He didn't ask, simply held open the car door. I slid into the passenger seat with butterflies in my belly like I'd not experienced in a long time. This was the closest I'd been to Anakin in days.

A man who featured in my masturbatory fantasies. A guy who could provide sexual relief. If he wanted me.

I wasn't sure he did. I don't think I'd ever had a sexual encounter where I was fully sober. Most of my sexual escapades occurred in clubs, alleys, or bathrooms. Only rarely did I make it with a guy to bed. As for dating anyone? I could never be bothered, so I had no idea what to expect. What would Anakin do? What did I want? Sleeping with my boss? Bad idea. I'd gotten fired for it before mostly because I was usually a one-time-and-done kind of gal.

"You're thinking way too hard," he remarked as he drove.

"It's been that kind of day."

"I'm sure Sonja's going to do her best to push off the date of the Choosing."

"And if she can't?"

Rather than reply to that, he said, "Your lizard won't stop staring at me."

Polkie had clambered into the car the moment I opened the passenger door. He chose to ride on the dash, tail up, hunched, and if I didn't know better, glaring at my boss.

"I think it's your leather seats. He's not crazy about skin products." Made me glad I no longer had those snakeskin boots.

"He's too small to make anything useful." Not the best reply and probably why my gecko peed in retaliation.

"Ack! What the fuck?" Anakin swore.

"Touch my Polkie and die."

"I'd rather you touched me," he muttered.

Surely, I'd misunderstood, given how intently he stared at the road.

I'd still not figured him out. What was he? "Vampire."

"What?"

"You must be a vampire."

He chuckled. "And how did you come to that conclusion?"

"Well, for one, I usually only see you after dark." That first encounter had been dark, overcast.

"Because that's when my store is busiest. I'm more of a night person."

"Do you sparkle in sunlight?"

That brought a snort. "No. I'm not a vampire."

"Then what?"

"And ruin the surprise? I'm sure you'll figure it out eventually."

"Ugh. Why must everyone keep secrets?"

"Don't you have any?"

"Nope. Ask me anything."

"Do you miss the old you?"

"Wow, come out swinging, why don't you?" I paused and thought about it. "No. Which I'll admit is surprising. When I was in that lifestyle, getting wasted all the time, doing what I wanted, with no regard for anyone, I thought that I was living my best life."

"And now?"

"Now, I realize I was just hiding. Pretending to be happy when, in reality, I was miserable and lonely." A loneliness that would hit me again if Sonja truly did leave.

"You're sad all of a sudden."

"Sad and afraid. What if, with Sonja gone, I fall back into my bad habits?"

"Do you want to?"

"No."

"Then don't."

"Says a man who hasn't struggled with addiction," I grumbled.

"Which shows how little you know." He reached for something in the console of his car and flicked it to me.

A coin with five years stamped on it.

I frowned. "Isn't that an AA token? But I saw you drink in your office."

"It wasn't booze I was addicted to."

"Then what?"

The car pulled to a stop, and rather than answer, he turned toward me. "You won't be alone."

"You can't know that for sure."

"I can because I'll be there with you, if you want me."

Want him? Was he oblivious to my lusting?

I spilled from his car, needing the night air before I did something I couldn't take back, like throw myself at my boss and kiss him.

He probably meant what he said as a friend. Friends didn't fuck, because sex changed everything.

"Was it something I said?" he asked, reaching my side.

"You should go home. I'll be fine."

"What if I don't want to leave?"

I glanced at him. His gaze remained intent on me. Not the stare of a friend.

He dragged me close, and his lips pressed against mine.

He was my boss. This would change everything. I really shouldn't allow it.

But I was a healthy—and, yes, horny—woman who kissed him right back.

It might have gone further if not for Sonja's hollered, "Get in here so I can say goodbye."

23

"What do you mean you're leaving?" I sounded like a whiny child, wringing my hands as I followed her from her workshop to her room as she packed a suitcase. Anakin remained downstairs.

"I've been called."

"So I've heard. And what, they can't wait a few days?"

"I'm needed urgently."

"I need you."

She paused, her expression somber. "I wish I had more time to teach you, but it appears that you're to follow the same path I did."

"What's that supposed to mean?"

"I also lost my mentor too soon and was thrust into the pot before ready."

"Fuck the pot. I'm not even a chopped vegetable. You've barely begun teaching me."

"You have the basics, just like I did, and will keep learning. Magic is about more than perfect patterns; it's about intent. You'll find what works for you."

"In time for this Choosing ceremony?"

Her lips pressed tight. "I'm going to do my best to delay it."

"Damian seems to think it will be soon."

"Damian is a demon with a forked tongue. Don't listen to him. Trust yourself, Faye."

Trust myself? How could I when I'd spent so long making the wrong choices?

I trailed Sonja downstairs and met Anakin at the bottom. We stood together as Sonja put on her coat and shoes while giving me some final instructions.

"The house is yours. Keep your room or change it. That's up to you. The rest of my things will be packed and sent to my new home within the week. Don't worry about the bills. They will be covered. Food delivered. You'll just have to worry about paying for the extras you want."

"You're assuming I'll be the next witch of the city and not tossed out when I lose."

An air hand slapped me.

"Enough of the negativity. You will succeed because there is no other choice. Goodbye, Faye."

Sonja hugged me, then Anakin, before leaving.

I hugged myself, feeling the tremble in my limbs. The fear in my heart. The dryness in my mouth.

In the past, when my anxiety got this bad, I'd have found a way to dull it. Pills. Booze. A combination of.

That was old Faye.

New Faye had risen from the dead. Had magic. Potential. And a fucking demon to beat.

I glanced at Anakin.

"Want to watch me set shit on fire?"

24

I'd like to say I set Anakin ablaze. Or his clothes, at least. However, he wasn't kidding when he said he wanted to help me. We spent the rest of the first night practicing my fire and protection spells in the workshop.

When my fatigue had me almost setting the book I studied on fire, Anakin sent me to bed.

And by bed, he meant alone.

He left, and it was just me in the house.

A warm little body crawled onto my chest. Polkie snuggled, and I felt less afraid. Less alone. I slept.

I dreamed.

I dreamed I was in a warehouse, a big, empty one, facing off against a woman. Blonde-haired, blue-eyed. Cute and perky. I knew it had to be Yolanthe.

She wielded a silver wand and traced beautiful, intricate patterns in the air. Each one executed perfectly.

I saw no one else but a deep voice said, "Proceed."

My turn. I held up a wooden stick, the kind that appeared as if I'd grabbed it off the ground. Ridged and crooked. My designs were decent, but nothing close to Yolanthe's perfection.

Sweat trickled down my forehead as the next round got more complicated.

While I couldn't see anyone, I heard the whispers. The jeering. The judging and the mockery.

Triumph lit Yolanthe's expression. I began to lose focus, and my work got sloppy. The blowback rocked me, and a hush fell before a buzz of sound with words emerged from it.

"Failure."

"Washed-up druggie."

"Trash."

"Failure. How did you think you could ever be good enough?"

Maybe if I'd had more time. If only Sonja didn't have to leave.

If only you believed in yourself.

I emerged from the dream with a sob, my heart racing and my T-shirt damp with sweat.

Why did even my subconscious plague me?

Rising from my bed, I went to the bathroom and stared at myself in the mirror. I looked like always. Pink hair. Nose ring. Dark circles under my eyes. But they were from lack of sleep, not a hangover.

As for the rest...I looked good. I'd lost the gauntness that'd plagued me because I forgot to eat. My skin, while pale, shone with health. Amazing what a few weeks had done.

So what if I wasn't ready for this Choosing ritual? I'd accomplished a lot, and I could... No, I *would* keep working hard because this was the kind of person I wanted to be. Not one stealing to supply a drug habit. Not the raucous drunk that no one wanted around.

I wanted to be the Faye that answered a knock at the door and saw Leslie standing there with a shy smile and a paper bag.

"Hey," I said.

"Hey, right back." She bit her lower lip before blurting out, "I heard what happened with Sonja. I was wondering if I could help."

"You know magic?"

She shook her head. "Not really, but the Choosing isn't just about that. Sometimes, there's fighting."

My brows rose. "Excuse me?"

"The Urban Witch shouldn't be afraid to tackle threats for the city. So, yeah, combat skills are a plus."

"No one mentioned that part," I muttered.

"I can teach you some moves."

"You?" I could tell I'd hurt her feelings with my incredulity. It made me feel like an asshole. "I'm sorry. It's just... You don't look like the brawling type."

Her cheeks dimpled as she smiled. "I'm actually a black belt. I grew up in a rough neighborhood."

"If you're willing to teach, then I'm willing to learn. Where should we go to practice?"

After the breakfast she'd brought, we ended up going to a local gym because they had mats to cushion my falls. My many, *many* falls.

Leslie might appear innocuous, but she knew her shit. I flew more times than I wanted to count. But after a few hours, I learned to block and counter.

However, I'd taken a beating to get to that point. I groaned as we returned to the house, my body aching with bruises and sore muscles.

Which was when Leslie introduced me to a special salve that proved easy to make. Add in a bit of magic and presto. I felt—"Good as new!" I stretched and smiled as my aches and pains eased.

"Told you it would work," she crowed.

"Thank you."

"No biggie." She blushed.

"Let me make you dinner." I had no idea what to cook, but I'd figure something out.

Leslie shook her head. "I gotta go. I'm covering Joni's shift tonight."

"Need a hand?"

"I'll be okay. Besides, you'll probably want to study."

Actually, I didn't, but I would.

Book in my lap, I chilled in the living room with Polkie on my shoulder, when a knock sounded.

Could it be Anakin?

I sprang to answer, but only as I pulled open the door, and my gecko hissed, did I realize my stupidity.

A blonde woman stood on the step. Beautiful, just like in my dream.

"You're Yolanthe."

"And you're..." She paused as she eyed me up and down. "Interesting."

The comment was meant to shame me, to shrink me in size. My chin lifted. I'd spent my life being different. She'd have to try harder.

"And you're the apprentice who failed."

Her lips pinched. "I didn't fail. I pursued a different opportunity."

"With a demon." My lip curled. "Hardly something to brag about."

She lost her annoyed look to purr, "Spoken by someone who has no idea of the pleasures to be found."

"Hey, if you like evil dick, then cool for you. Me, I'll stick to my own kind."

She laughed, like the tinkle of tiny bells. "Now there's a lie if I've heard one. Rumor has it Anakin is your lover."

"He's not." But not for lack of wanting.

"Has he told you yet what he is? What he can do?"

"No, but I guess you're about to."

"And ruin the surprise?" Her lips curved into an evil smile.

"Is there a point for this visit?" I asked.

"Just wanted to meet you before the Choosing. To see for myself who I'm up against." Again, she eyed me with disdain. "I see Damian was right. I have nothing to worry about."

"Don't be so sure of that." Anakin's deep voice from behind me startled, but I didn't let it show. He must have snuck in the back.

"Should have known you'd be lurking. When at first you don't succeed, try, try again," Yolanthe sang.

"Go away, Yolanthe," Anakin demanded.

She smirked instead. "Have you seen the scar on his thigh yet? Ask him how he got it, and you'll find out exactly what he is."

Wait, how did she know about…? The realization hit me.

Anakin had slept with her. Sonja's former protégé.

And now, he played nice with me.

The door slammed shut, and he sighed.

"It's not what you think."

I whirled and arched a brow. "So, you're not like Damian, trying to seduce the next potential Urban Witch?"

"Oh, I'm planning to seduce you, but not because of your future role."

"You going to claim an undying passion for me?" Because I'd never believe it.

"More like lust. I've wanted to fuck you from the moment you insulted me." He took a step closer. "I've wanted to grab you by the hair and nibble at that mouth of yours. Strip off your shirt and play with those rings on your nipples. I want to yank them and hear you cry out as I'm fucking you deep and hard."

Oh. My.

Yeah. My panties were drenched. But I did have *some* self-respect.

Barely.

"I won't be used." I shook my head, but temptation lingered. I had to distract myself. "What are you?"

"Something rare and reviled."

"Reviled? Why?"

"Because what I can do is considered dirty magic."

"If it's so dirty, why is Sonja your friend?"

"She wasn't for a while. After someone close to me died, I was lost for a bit. Depraved. As bad as Damian. Maybe even worse."

"You were grieving."

"Grieving makes it sound noble. I was anything but."

"What did you do?" I asked.

He raked a hand through his hair and paced away from me. "You keep asking what I am. The simple explanation is a warlock."

"You do magic like me?"

"I do magic, but it's nothing like yours. Your base element appears to be fire."

"What's yours?"

"Spirit."

I frowned. "Meaning, what?"

"I can manipulate the spirits of living things."

My expression must have shown my confusion, because he sighed. "I'm a necromancer."

"Holy shit, you're a zombie maker."

He winced. "That would be the crude version of my skills."

"What's the better term, then?"

"Necromancer."

"Duh. I meant, what does it entail? Does it have anything to do with your sprinkle special?"

"Yes." He pinched his lips before saying, "I can take life and inject it into other things. Those who ingest it will see their vitality improved."

The sprinkle special. "You sell the fountain of youth!"

"A temporary thing that doesn't last, but that doesn't stop people from buying."

"Hold on a second. You said you take life. Where do you get it from?"

"There is no shortage of those seeking death or those who deserve it."

"I'm confused. Why did she make it sound like a bad thing?"

"Because remember the grief I spoke of?" I nodded, and he continued, his expression bleak. "I was in love a long time ago."

"I take it that it didn't end well."

"Someone killed Kyla. And not just her but also our unborn child." His lips turned down, and his expression became vacant as he told me. "I was devastated."

"You brought them back to life."

His mouth twisted. "I used my necromancy to revive Kyla. The baby was another matter. Even I knew better than to do something so abominable."

"I take it the resurrection didn't go well."

"Kyla had been dead too long by the time I attempted. Her spirit had fled. The damage to her body was too extensive. It didn't matter how much life I poured in; it wasn't enough. But that didn't stop me. And to fuel the never-ending flow I needed, I went on a rampage, trying to find out who'd killed them."

"Did you find the person responsible?"

"No. And at one point in my grief, it didn't matter. Because I needed lives to keep Kyla functioning."

"How long?" I asked. How long had he fallen into a pit of despair?

"Almost seven years. Years of me killing to keep my dead lover alive. Given I couldn't stay in one place for long, I had to move often. That's how I ended up here, where I met Sonja."

I thought of what Yolanthe had said about the scar on his leg. "She stabbed you to bring you to your senses."

He laughed, a sad and ugly thing. "Not her. Kyla. You see, while I'd reanimated her body, I couldn't bring back her soul. The thing that made her the woman I loved. Sonja thought she could help me. She prayed to her goddess and was answered. Kyla's soul returned to the body I'd kept alive. Only it wasn't the woman I used to know. Dying...changes a person. Or perhaps I never saw her true self. Whatever the answer, she wasn't the same. She returned cruel. Bent on vengeance for her death and the loss of our child. She hated me. Everyone. When I tried to stop her from decimating every living thing, she stabbed me." He put a hand to his thigh. "She made me realize just how wrong I'd been."

It hit me, and I said softly, "Which is when she had to die again." But by his hand.

He nodded. "The grief hit me a second time, but so did guilt at the evil I'd wrought in the name of love. It was Sonja who helped me redirect that negativity into something positive. Who helped remind me of the woman I loved and not the monster I'd made her into."

"How does the bakery fit into this?"

His head inclined. "Kyla always said she wanted to own one. At the time, I'd been less than kind in my mockery of the idea. It turned out that baking soothed me. Turned me away from my other predilections."

"That five-year token is for not raising the dead."

A smile ghosted around his lips. "Zombie free for almost eight now."

"Congrats?" I arched a brow.

He snorted. "Is that all you have to say?"

"Let me guess, when you were dating Yolanthe, she found out and wasn't enthused."

"Hardly dating. She pursued me. I rejected her,

but her ego couldn't handle it. When Damian revealed what I'd done, she called me a monster."

"That's kind of priceless given she turned around and dated the demon dude."

He shrugged. "I'm sure his influence had something to do with it."

"Gotta say, not sure why the whole necromancy thing is a big deal. I mean, yeah, you can raise dead people, but if it makes you feel better, I can cremate them if you do."

"You don't have to pretend. Necromancy is probably one of the most abhorred of the magical arts."

"I don't know. I mean, seems kind of cool to me. Imagine the Halloween display we could put on. Is it only people you can animate? Or animals, too?"

He blinked at me. "Are you joking about it?"

"Would you rather I flip out?"

"No."

"I mean, I can hardly cast any stones. Have you seen how many things I've accidentally burned down?"

"You didn't kill people."

"Not true. Pretty sure I killed that one guy who came after me at Sonja's shop."

He waved a hand. "Red Caps are scum. I drain them of their essence happily."

"Now who's trying to make me feel better?"

His wry smile tugged at something inside me.

Hot and emotionally wounded. Could he get any sexier?

"Wanna screw?" I asked without any subtlety.

His jaw dropped.

Who knew what might have happened if someone hadn't knocked on the damned door?

25

What the fuck was it with people constantly interrupting?

"You going to answer?" he asked.

"Rather not." I scowled at the offending door and whoever stood beyond it. My gut knotted, knowing it wouldn't be good. However, avoiding the things that were tough wouldn't make them go away.

The door opened with a simple yank, and I looked upon a strange sight. A short creature, feline in appearance but standing on two legs, wearing livery that belonged in a more regal century.

"To the witch known as Faye Bronson." The feline then offered me an envelope, cream-colored and sealed. Pressed into the hardened wax, an intricate symbol.

I pressed the pad of my thumb to it, and the seal evaporated, the letter unfolded, and the symbols on it swirled to life, forming a voice.

"Present yourself, on the night of no moon, for the Choosing. Failure to show is death."

"Let me guess, fail to win and I die, too," I muttered.

Message delivered, the feline turned to leave.

"Excuse me, but your little message there failed to give an address."

The feline paused and glanced at me over its shoulder. "Where the magic is strongest." Its tone indicated that should be obvious.

"How do I find it?"

"Magic," was the snorted reply as the feline hit the sidewalk and disappeared. Literally.

Well, shit.

I didn't realize I muttered aloud until Anakin said, "Guess we'll have to work harder. We don't have much time."

What I really wanted to do was find a great big joint, smoke it, and become a vegetable for the day eating potato chips.

Which would do absolutely nothing to help me.

Ugh.

I sighed. "Where should we start?"

Apparently, he thought I needed defense training. Not the hand-to-hand combat kind—I would have enjoyed that, especially the pinning part. Anakin asked me to use my magic to attack and defend.

Given we stood in the living room, I eyed him askance. "You want me to fling fireballs in the house?"

"Actually, the circle upstairs might be better. It will prevent any collateral damage."

"That's tight quarters for a magical blast."

"Most fights are close."

A grimace tugged my lips. "Don't blame me then if you lose your pretty hair."

He grinned. "You're assuming I can't defend myself."

I suddenly worried. "Are you going to throw zombies at me?" Could he summon dead people from afar?

"Guess you'll soon find out."

We went upstairs into the protective circle with its magical star at the center. Entering it was like walking into a muffling bubble.

For some reason, I dropped into a fighter stance, knees slightly bent, hands loose at my sides.

Anakin appeared more relaxed, a slight smirk around his lips. "Give it to me."

"Isn't that supposed to be my line?"

"Are you asking me to seduce you?"

"Actually, to fuck me. I'm not into romance." At least, I hadn't been until now. Anakin, though, intrigued me. He might be worth a couple of romps. But even once would change the dynamic between us.

"Fucking is for animals." He flicked his hand, and suddenly, a bull made of wind and blue light materialized, charging for me.

Cool. But I'd had enough lessons to recognize the illusion.

I lifted my hand and pushed against it, shattering the construct. "Aren't people simply animals further along in evolution?"

"Sentience makes us different. We feel." Another twist of his hand, and ghostly arms wrapped around me, cold enough to chatter my teeth.

Fire burned within me, and I let it roll out of my body, evaporating the frozen hold. "Beasts can feel."

"But do they have a connection that transcends flesh?" He suddenly stood before me, looking down, and my heart stopped.

Sarcasm died in my throat because I had no

breath to say anything.

The kiss was enough to rock me. My arms wound around his neck.

His around my torso.

We kissed in our little bubble and ended up on the floor. Our clothes scattered. Flesh rubbed against flesh.

His mouth remained latched to mine, claiming one moment, surrendering to my tongue the next.

His hands stroked me, squeezing a breast and rolling the tip. Slipping between my thighs to find me wet and wanting.

When he held himself over me, his eyes glinted. Wild with passion.

For me.

My lips curved as I reached for him.

He thrust into me, and I gasped, filled with his steely strength. I clung to him as we rocked to a primal rhythm.

Each striving for a pinnacle just out of reach.

We arrived together, my body tightening, as did his, our climaxes exploding and leaving me limp and breathless. Sated, and yet throbbing.

So good.

"So good," he whispered.

But the second time was even better.

26

THE SEX ENDED THE MAGIC PRACTICE FOR THE night. Instead, we fucked...I didn't know how many times. Each time I wanted to sing a certain Madonna song. It was just that good.

Incredible.

But when I woke, my body pleasantly tingling, I knew it was time to buckle down. I had work to do before the Choosing.

The mattress held Anakin's imprint, but not his actual body. I poured myself out of bed and hit the shower. A toothbrush was a must, as well.

I emerged into the bedroom to find it still empty. Had he left?

It would be ironic since I was usually the one sneaking out of beds.

I headed downstairs and heard the murmur of voices from the kitchen. It held not just Anakin and Leslie but someone new, as well.

An old lady, her hair pure white, the wrinkles on her face too many to count. Her eyes were a sharp blue, though.

"Morning." Anakin had a soft greeting for me as he tugged the chair by his side for me to sit.

I slid into it as Leslie said, "Sorry to be here so early. I heard the news." The news being the Choosing date being set.

"Guess it's almost win or die time." I tried for light and nonchalant. Did they suspect the anxiety inside?

"Most likely die," was the old lady's opinion.

It earned her a scowl. "Thanks for the vote of confidence."

"Surely, there's something you can do to help her?" Leslie queried.

The crone eyed me and shook her head. "She's too new. Just look at her. She can't even contain her magic."

The rebuke had me slapping a hand over my wrist missing the hair bracelet charm. "I'm trying."

"No try. Do."

"Was that supposed to be a Yoda imitation?" I asked, heading for the coffee.

"You brought me here to waste my time, I see." The old lady rose from her chair.

Anakin did, as well. "You know I wouldn't have asked if I didn't believe she could succeed."

Once more, she subjected me to a hard stare. I sipped my coffee rather than give the old broad the finger.

"She does have a strong core of power. But does she have the ability to control it?"

"I've gotten better," I muttered.

"Better isn't good enough. You need to be able to react, adapt, change on the fly," the crone snapped.

"Are we switching to hockey analogies now?" I just couldn't help myself.

"Impertinent. You don't seem to grasp the gravity."

"And you're going to show me, I suppose?"

The old lady didn't move. Yet I knew the wave of force aimed at me was courtesy of her. It took every inch of will inside me not to flinch as I countered her magic. I imagined the shield spell, better able to visualize it than draw it.

Not something I'd tried on a large scale before.

Because, surely, if spells could be as simple as a witch thinking of a pattern, everyone would do it. My small experiments had worked thus far, but a shield was much larger and needed a little more oomph.

I saw the gold-embossed symbols transposed over the scene before me, the lines deepening and taking a more tri-dimensional state.

The force spell spilled up on it.

I took a casual sip of coffee to hide my trembling relief.

"How did you do that? Did you help her?" the crone accused.

"Not me." Anakin raised his hands.

"What happened?" Leslie exclaimed.

"She visualized the spell well enough to hold it and make it work."

"Doesn't everyone?" I asked.

"No. Most are too easily distracted, and it falls apart." The old lady eyed me. "You might be more interesting than I thought."

A slight smirk tugged my lips.

I paid for it later when the old lady schooled me in the circle.

Thinking spells was easy when you had time and no distraction. Hammered in numerous directions at once proved harder.

I emerged from that training depressed and in need of a bath. I settled for a hot shower and guzzled the hot cocoa Anakin brought me.

He sat on the edge of the bed. "I think you impressed Morrigan."

The name did not suit her. It should have been tougher. Something like Brass Lady. Or Wrinkled Widow.

"She wiped the floor with my ass so many times, I might never be able to sit properly again."

"Don't feel bad. Morrigan has decades of experience on you. The reason she's still alive is because she doesn't lose."

"Is that supposed to make me feel better?" A grimace wiped with a sip of my hot cocoa.

"I know what will actually work."

It involved a massage, epic sex, and snuggling.

The next day, I expected a repeat of my humiliation, but Morrigan instead sat cross-legged in the circle. She pointed to a spot in front of her.

"Sit."

I plopped down. "What's on the menu today?"

"Take off the bracelet."

The charm that hid me from those who might think I was delicious. I tugged it free and tossed it aside.

"Are you going to even try to hide your light?" grumbled my teacher.

"What light?" I glanced down at myself. I didn't see it.

"This one." Morrigan suddenly turned bright. But not the kind that made you squint.

Her magic was like a warm, delicious caramel for my senses. I wanted to eat her all up.

As I reached for it, she snapped a shield down.

I blinked. I was sad. I'd never even gotten a bite. "Is that what I am to those who can see my magic? Candy?"

"You are ambrosia, more so now I'll wager than when you were given the power. And it will only get stronger as you develop."

"I don't know how to mask my flavor." My nose wrinkled.

"Hide it."

"How?"

"Any way that works."

Before I could whine, because I was stalling, something latched on. Not to my body but my magic. It nibbled on it, and I was horrified. It pulled at me. I could feel it. It hurt, but not a pain of the body. It was like someone chewing on my soul.

"Stop," I asked to no avail. Morrigan kept tugging

on me. "I said stop!" I thought of a wall of fire, surrounding me. It rose in a blue-white shimmer that caused a hiss as Morrigan recoiled.

Rather than be pissed that I'd cut off her source of candy, she smiled. "About time you figured out how to shield, although you might want to opt for something a little less dramatic."

Given I could see the flames dancing around me, I understood her point. It took a little concentration to make them invisible, and I had to keep thinking about it to keep it up, I soon noticed.

"Practice will make it like breathing."

"Breathing is a normal function," I grumbled as my shield wobbled.

"Are you arguing with me again?"

"No." I worked on keeping up my shield. "This won't be easy during a fight."

"Then let it shine. It will distract your opponent. Just be sure to act fast if you do. Many stronger than you would gladly suck you dry." Morrigan rose to her feet. "I'm hungry. I'm going to see what's lurking in the neighborhood."

I almost asked if she was going to hunt mutant rats or something, only I worried at her reply.

As I headed for the kitchen, I found Leslie,

buttering bread for grilled cheese. "Where's Anakin?" I asked.

"Store business. He says he'll be back in time for the Choosing tonight."

I would have liked to say I'd forgotten it was today. That would be a lie. I remained aware of the ticking hours and minutes down to this ritual. I wasn't ready.

I had no choice. It made my anxiety do back flips of agitation. Instead of reaching for ketchup for dipping, I wanted a bottle of hooch or a pot-laced cigarette.

Those were crutches to avoid the things that scared me. I didn't need them to face life, but I could have used someone to hold my hand.

The time of the Choosing approached, with no Anakin, no Morrigan, and no clue where I had to go.

Even Leslie appeared worried. "I don't know where he is. He's not answering his phone."

The sense of running out of time had me faking a smile. "I don't need him. I don't need anybody."

False bravado. Wearing a mishmash of colors—rather than my preferred funeral black—I left Sonja's house and hit the sidewalk, wondering which way to go.

Find the magic, indeed. Leslie stood behind me, apparently blind to it, despite her tail.

As a kid, there was only one way to decide things.

Eeny. Meeny. Miny. Moe.

It chose right. I took one step and saw Polkie in my way. He flicked his tongue.

I whirled around.

Left it was, then.

As I started striding, Polkie chose to ride my shoulder, invisible to my friend. Was it cheating to have his tongue flicking me, giving me aid when I hesitated at street corners?

It would be worse to miss my appointment with Fate.

The horror movie lover in me appreciated the classic blacked-out warehouse I found myself outside of an hour or so later. The anxious woman within warned what a bad idea entering would be.

No shit.

No choice.

"Want me to see if anyone is here?" Leslie offered. Bless her brave damned heart. How had I managed to make myself a friend?

"Doesn't really matter if there is or not. I'm supposed to be here."

Run away.

Go. Now.

You can't do this.

Fuck you, doubt. I threw back my shoulders and faked courage. After all, I'd managed to be brave when drunk. It wasn't booze that made me able to do it but attitude.

I can do this.

Had to.

The door opened, and I stepped into a dark place. The entrance slammed shut behind me, and I suddenly blinked as bright light flooded.

The space loomed. Massive. Shaped in a long rectangle, at least fifty feet across, probably a hundred or more deep. Pillars rose in metal monoliths from concrete footings, latching into a roof where it peaked. At its highest probably a good three stories.

Roof trusses added extra support, although I had to wonder if they'd hold given the spectators perched upon them.

No one mentioned there would be an audience. Then again, I should have known. People loved a good fight. And, apparently, Cryptozoids did, too. I saw little signs of humanity among the crowd. Plenty of wings and horns, though, along with leathery skin, extra limbs, and an aura of magic that daunted.

Fuck.

Fuck.

Fuck.

A nudge had me moving my feet, heading for where the light shone the brightest. Polkie scurried ahead of me, his form fading until I walked alone.

A dais held several chairs. Not all of them occupied. Those that held someone...

I held my breath. These weren't mere people. Could this be the famed Pantheon?

One of them eyed me, a woman with green hair that undulated as if caught in a watery ripple. "Who presents themselves?" A sonorous demand.

"Faye." No last name. No title. Because I was just me.

"You are late."

"No one mentioned a time." Yes, I argued. Because it wouldn't have killed them to include an address with their threatening invite.

"The time of the Choosing is well known."

"Apparently, not. Anyhow, I'm here. What's next?"

Her reply was for the audience, given she glanced upward, and her voice emerged loud enough for all to hear. "It is the time of the Choosing. Who will best serve this city and its citizens?"

The question wasn't directed at me, and yet I couldn't help but reply. "Is getting witches to fight really the best indicator of who should get the job of Urban Witch?" I asked, causing the most unnatural hush.

"You dare argue about ritual?"

"Well, yeah, when it seems out of touch with the times."

"This is not a time for stupid questions. We have a ceremony to perform."

"And how long have you been performing it? Have you wondered if it's maybe outdated? The world is changing. Sometimes, old rituals need to, as well."

She stared at me, everyone in those special chairs did, incredulous enough that the guy with eyes on slender stalks whispered, "She's completely insane." Then, with pleasure. "I like her."

The woman giving the speech didn't. "This is how it's done. If you don't like it, leave."

"And forfeit? Not happening. I can do this." Sonja believed in me. Leslie, too. Even Anakin must, given he'd helped me practice. I wasn't about to give up.

"Then enter the ring and let us see who is chosen."

I'm proud to say I didn't pee myself walking into a wall of magic. I could be honest, though; it might have singed a little hair. But I made it inside and then paused as I saw Leslie within, along with Leroy.

"What are you doing here?" I asked.

"We're the first line you have to go through to make it to the next round." Leslie's lips turned down as she announced it.

"You're making me fight my friends?" I glanced around at the fuzzy dome that comprised the ring.

No reply.

Leslie advanced on me. I dropped into a stance she'd taught me.

"How long have you known you'd have to fight me?" I asked.

"I didn't. They snared me as I walked in and told me I had no choice."

As we spoke, Leroy flanked me. I'd better not lose track of him. We weren't close. He possibly wouldn't hesitate. As a quarter-elf, he didn't have enough magic to hurt me much, but that studded mace looked mighty painful.

"I don't want to hurt you." Leslie was my friend.

"Ditto." Leslie bit her lip. "But you need to win against us to go to the next round."

But did it need to be over her dead or injured body?

I couldn't do that, so I tried something else. I put her to sleep. It wasn't hard as it turned out. Her mind couldn't stop the spell I imagined flying at her. Leroy didn't fare any better. They both dropped to the ground.

There was a moment of quiet, and then the dome changed color. As it did, their bodies disappeared.

"First round complete. Both move on."

Both? Shit, that was a reminder this was a competition, and I couldn't fail.

I glanced around but couldn't see Yolanthe. Apparently, I wouldn't be allowed to watch and study my opponent. Bummer. But in good news, it seemed killing wasn't required to win rounds.

Yet.

The dome went dark, the kind that even blinking didn't dispel. When light returned, it proved low and somber. Anakin strode from the shadows.

"No." I shook my head. They couldn't use him against me. We'd refuse.

He stopped in front of me. "Hello, Faye."

"I'm not going to fight you."

"You won't be able to put me to sleep like you did the others."

"Then what can I do? Because you don't want to fight me."

"I don't. But I also have a duty to this city. It has asked me to see if you're worthy to be the Urban Witch. Worthy to protect us all."

"You don't think I am." Why else would he stand against me?

"I think you're perfect, actually. My lover. When my armies of the dead march, you'll be by my side, watching."

"Wait, what are you talking about? What zombie army?"

"The one I shall use to take over. First this state. And then, as the bodies multiply, we'll spread." He waved his hand. "With you as my partner, none shall be able to prevail."

I stared at my lover who'd just offered to make me his zombie queen. I had no doubt that together we could cause some serious havoc.

No.

I sauntered closer. "Is this your way of asking me to be your wife?"

He smiled at me. "As if I would have anyone

else." His arm snaked around me, and I stood on tiptoe and whispered, "I know you aren't the real Anakin." Because I knew his story. He'd told me his past. I'd seen the pain his actions caused. He'd never descend into that kind of killing again.

"It could be real," he whispered insidiously. "You. Me. We could be emperors of the world."

"No thanks. Sounds like a lot of work."

I shoved away from Anakin, and the illusion disappeared. The dome turned clear, and I saw Anakin right away, standing behind magical bars keeping him, Leslie, and even the other store staff locked away.

Because they didn't want them helping me. Well, shucks, I was flattered they thought people cared enough to try.

Bad news for the testers, though. I was onto their dirty tricks. I could have been pissed, but I understood what they did. They were testing my moral compass. Commendable, actually.

Even more awesome? I'd passed with flying colors. It resulted in a little more faith in myself. "What's next?"

"Death," was the only hissed warning before a magical force hit me from behind.

27

I no sooner got smacked than I found myself in that dark place.

Uh-oh. Had I died again?

Not dead. A familiar presence did that weird speaking thing with me.

"If I'm not dead, then why are we chatting?" A cold fear hit me. "Are you taking back the magic?"

A gift cannot be returned.

A slight relief. "Why am I here then?" And why could I better understand the entity this time?

You're here because you let down your guard.

"That cow clocked me from behind."

And? the presence mocked.

"Wake me up then. I'll fight." And dirty, given my opponent started it.

Wake yourself.

"Smart-mouthed deity," I grumbled as I willed myself to wake.

I opened my eyes just as my face kissed the pavement. Ouch. But in good news, I'd not been gone that long. Not even a blink, so ignoring the pain in my cheek, I rose and whirled.

Yolanthe smirked, dressed in black leather, looking ultra cool compared to me in my ripped jeans and T-shirt, bright pink with yellow lettering saying *Fuck off*. A gift from Leslie.

At least, I knew now that this test was fake. The judges watched what I'd do. I waved my hand. "Are we still playing charades?"

"I'm real, you ignorant twat." Yolanthe tossed her hair.

"Prove it."

Her foot swung so fast, I didn't react, and it connected with my hip.

I sucked in a breath, to her pleased chuckle.

"Real enough for you? I will give you kudos, though. I'm surprised you showed up. Even more that you made it this far. I didn't take you for a killer."

"You killed through your previous rounds?" I gaped. How had she passed?

She rolled her shoulders. "I have to win."

"At what cost?"

"Any." A firm reply.

Meaning she'd murder me in a heartbeat. Problem being, I had no interest in actually killing her. It offered a dilemma; how to subdue her? With her magic, I wouldn't be able to put her to sleep. Just like I doubted she'd simply surrender.

How could I win against Yolanthe in a way that didn't cause her permanent harm?

I had no idea as she flung the first burst of magic at me. Given I'd watched her drawing the spell, with her handy-dandy wand, I'd known it was coming. I dodged it easily and sent back a burst of fireballs by pointing my finger to focus. Little ones she easily knocked aside. Maybe I should have remembered to bring a wand.

Too late now. I needed to buy time to figure out a plan. She gave me no quarter.

She advanced on me, silver wand in one fist. The other held a chain of some sort with a dangling pendant. She waved them both. Ambidextrous spell casting.

Cool.

I split my mind into two to cast my visual counter versions.

The mirror I conjured reflected her offensive spell, causing it to spark. She yelped as the backlash singed her shoulder, taking some hair as it passed.

"How?" she sputtered as she whirled into another combination. I managed to block each of them, but I tired.

She, on the other hand, kept going. "You'll never win. I'll haunt you forever. Because I am the Chosen. I will be the Urban Witch of this city."

It hit me then. "Can't be a witch without magic." I rushed her as I murmured it, because Anakin was right. A fight couldn't help but occur in close quarters.

My hands grabbed hold of Yolanthe, enough to bring us face to face. So close, I could almost kiss her. Instead, I sent out an etheric tongue.

I projected it past her shields to the candy core of her. I wanted to take her magic. Wanted to eat it so badly. But that would hurt her. So, instead, I did something possibly crueler. I severed her contact with it. I encased her magic, the ability to draw upon it, in a cocoon created by lacing strands of fire. Flames that needed no fuel to burn and didn't harm flesh. A fiery shield that she couldn't extinguish without magic.

She froze.

Horrified.

Relieved.

She stumbled from me with wide eyes. "What have you done?"

I'd blocked her use of magic, and the inevitable path she'd followed because of it.

She trembled and then whispered, "I'm free." She smiled. "Free."

"Fight, you stupid cunt!" Damian shouted.

"Silence!" The command came with a snap of fingers that made Damian pop out of sight. Hopefully, to somewhere warm and brimstony.

I might have been the only person who heard Yolanthe whisper, "Good riddance." As she turned to walk away, a bolt of light hit her, sending her to the floor.

Shocked, I turned and gaped at the presiding woman still holding out her weaponized finger, who preceded to order, "Take her away."

I didn't remain silent. "Why did you kill Yolanthe? She wasn't a threat to anyone."

"She's not dead. Just sleeping. When she wakes, she'll be a new person with no memories of this life."

"Oh." That actually sounded really perfect.

"Did you really think us bloodthirsty killers?"

"Yes."

"And yet you chose to not cause harm." My judge grinned, and her face shifted for a moment into a familiar one.

"Sonja?"

My old teacher smiled. "I can see why the city chose you."

"Wait a second, does that mean I won?"

"Indeed, you have. Congratulations. You are the new Urban Witch."

Shocked, I celebrated by face-planting again.

28

I managed to not bang my face during that faint, as a certain necromancer caught me.

"Thanks."

"Pretty sure you don't want to be sporting bruises for the official portrait that will be displayed in the next edition of the Cryptonews," was his wry reply.

"Really thinking you have a hero complex, Mr. Wants to Zombie the World."

He winced. "I can't believe they did that. As if I'd ever tell anyone my plan."

I laughed. "As plans went, it was almost appealing." My lover and me ruling together, forever.

"Yet you resisted."

"Dude, running one city will keep me busy. How

would I manage more and still get enough sex on the side?"

"Not to mention, you'll need a job to buy things."

"Wait, are you telling me the witch gig doesn't pay?"

"Not in actual coin you can use in the real world. Which means, you need to supplement."

I groaned. "Really not selling it to me."

"Want to back out?"

"No." I grinned. "Assuming I'm still employed, boss?"

"That's something we'll have to discuss, actually."

"You'd better not be firing me because we're having sex."

"Not firing you, but you're getting a promotion. You see, I am only half-owner. A silent partner owns the other half."

It took me only a second to breathe, "Holy shit, I inherited half the shop as the Urban Witch."

He winked. "Guess we'll be working closely together."

I couldn't wait, especially because I knew I wouldn't be alone.

EPILOGUE

Six months later...

Being the Urban Witch could be busy or boring, depending on the phase of the moon or the alignment of the planets. Renewing magics in protective charms proved the simplest part of my job, and I did it during my pastry shop hours. Anakin had his sprinkle special, and I had the icing delight. Although my payment for those magical services could be odd at times. I had jars of stuff that could apparently chew holes through flesh. But in good news, I'd traded the giant singing cockroach given by one happy client to someone with the most amazing hair dye.

When it came to defending the city, I'd learned a lot, like how not to explode waves of bugs pouring from sewers. One, blowing up stuff caused a mess, and two, it would take a while to forget all those twitching millipede legs in the aftermath. My gorge still rose at the reminder.

I did see Sonja from time to time, sometimes looking as I'd first met her, and others appearing like some otherworldly goddess. Apparently, she had some mermaid genes in her family. But the one thing that didn't change? Her bluntness, but also her pride in me.

I didn't tell her that being good wasn't easy.

Given I struggled at times with cravings, I took to attending AA meetings that I organized at the shop. Every Sunday night, those of us struggling with addiction met.

Leroy, with his obsessive need to know where his partner was at every moment of every day.

Menusa—related to the famous Medusa—with her head of serpents, struggling with her vegan diet. Her hair was less than impressed that they weren't even allowed to eat bugs.

Me, getting less obsessed with the loss of booze and dope and resisting, instead, the urge to eat magic—it really did tempt.

But I was stronger than my addictions.

Eventually, I reached the point in my recovery

and self-discovery where I had to make amends. I'd hurt and fucked over a lot of people in my life. No point in shying away from that fact. I'd probably never be able to apologize to most of the folks I'd screwed. But there were two people who'd suffered the most from the old, shitty me, and they deserved something.

Mom and Dad. I'd begun writing to my mom three months after I got clean. The words came with difficulty at first but penning them on paper helped me gather my thoughts and find the right apology rather than whining and giving excuses.

To my surprise, my mom wrote back. And then my dad started adding short notes to the missives. Last month, we'd progressed to phone calls where neither party hung up upset. We even laughed. Turned out my dad had a wry sense of humor.

It was going great until they asked to visit.

I wanted to scream that I wasn't ready. What if I disappointed them? I thought I'd come so far, but what if they didn't agree?

"It will be fine," Leslie reassured.

"Will it? Partially college-educated girl working in a pastry shop." That was all they could ever know. The other life I led, as half-business owner and Urban Witch, would have to remain hidden.

"Just don't offer them the garbage deluxe and it will be fine."

I wrinkled my nose. "I still say we should only be serving those in the alley." The reek sometimes had an unexpected and explosive side effect on other patrons.

Before Anakin could argue, my head swiveled. "They're here." I could have been the little girl in *Poltergeist* the way I muttered it.

"No matter, just remember I love you," Anakin murmured by my ear.

"I know." But I still wanted the love of my parents.

I almost fled to the kitchen, only to see Anakin standing in my path, arms crossed.

"Out of my way." I hyperventilated.

Anakin raised a brow. "No."

"I'm not ready."

Then it didn't matter because they were here, Mom and Dad, looking as hesitant as I felt.

What did they think seeing me? Because I still had the pink hair and piercings. One more tattoo since the last time I'd visited, as well. But I was also clear-eyed and sober.

As they neared the counter, I offered a soft, "Hey, Mom. Hi, Dad."

"Faye." My mother breathed my name, and I saw her tremble. I came around that counter quick and hugged her, an embrace we hadn't shared since I was a kid.

She sighed again. "I'm so glad you're back."

It had never occurred to me that she might have missed the little girl she'd raised and lost to selfishness. When we separated, she kept an arm around my waist.

I glanced shyly at my dad.

"You look good," my father stated. So did he.

"You lost weight," I remarked.

"No more beer." His lips turned down for a second. "Got me a new hobby."

"Bird watching," my mom said with a titter. "We're actually going on a road trip soon to follow the migration of some kind of swallow."

"That sounds fun."

"Would you like to come?" I heard the sincerity in the request. Which was enough for me.

"Can't. Gotta work, but I'd love daily updates. Maybe we could video chat so you can show me?"

As we indulged in idle chitchat, we took a seat in a booth. Leslie served us, while Anakin hovered at the cash register. My moral support if I faltered.

I worried for nothing.

When Leslie brought over a pie, I shyly stated, "I made it. Based off Grandma's special recipe."

Only as my mom took a bite and moaned did some of my tension ease. When she smiled at me and said, "It's just like she used to make," I almost fist-pumped.

My mom went to use the washroom, leaving me alone with my dad. I got tongue-tied. He didn't speak aloud either.

But he didn't remain completely quiet.

You prevailed.

I blinked at him.

Did you really think I'd let my only daughter die?

My mouth rounded.

He winked. *Don't tell your mother.*

Tell her what? That she might be married to some kind of pagan god?

Apparently, I'd always been special and had just been too dumb to recognize it.

I'd like to say that, from that moment on, Anakin and I lived happily ever after. We did. Kind of. But between those happy moments, there were stressful events, because bad guys were like weeds. I knew my parents were disappointed that Anakin and I chose not to have kids—at least not for the next few years—but we did adopt fur babies to love.

I just never told my mom that the giant dog whose belly she scratched was a Hellhound. And the cat? A glamoured miniature manticore, saved from a breeder who should have known better. As for Polkie, he remained by my side until he got a girlfriend and chose to move into the garage with her.

Hard to believe I'd turned my life around enough that I got to not only have an awesome career but also love.

And daily breakfast bacon because of a wager that Anakin lost.

Hope you enjoyed this little story inspired by a cover I just couldn't resist. Maybe one day we'll see a new story about the Urban Witch and her new job as protector of her city.

For more books or information see EveLanglais.com

www.ingramcontent.com/pod-product-compliance
Lightning Source LLC
LaVergne TN
LVHW031539060526
838200LV00056B/4576